**Alain Mabanckou** was born in 1966 in Congo. He currently lives in Los Angeles, where he teaches literature at UCLA. He received the Subsaharan African Literature Prize for *Blue-White-Red*, and the Prix Renaudot for *Memoirs of a Porcupine*, which is published by Serpent's Tail along with his earlier novels, *Broken Glass* and *African Psycho*.

### Praise for Alain Mabanckou

"This bar-room yarn-spinner tells his fellow tipplers' tales in a voice that swings between broad farce and aching tragedy. His farewell performance from a perch in Credit Gone West abounds in scorching wit and flights of eloquence . . . vitriolic comedy and pugnacious irreverence" Boyd Tonkin, *Independent*

"A dizzying combination of erudition, bawdy humour and linguistic effervescence" Melissa McClements, *Financial Times*

"*Broken Glass* is a comic romp that releases Mabanckou's sense of humour . . . Although its cultural and intertextual musings could fuel innumerable doctorates, the real meat of *Broken Glass* is its comic brio, and Mabanckou's jokes work the whole spectrum of humour" Tibor Fischer, *Guardian*

"Deserves the acclaim heaped upon it . . . self-mocking and ironic, a thought-provoking glimpse into a stricken country" *Waterstone's Books Quarterly*

"*Taxi Driver* for Africa's blank generation . . . a deftly ironic Grand Guignol, a pulp fiction vision of Frantz Fanon's 'wretched of the earth' that somehow manages to be both frightening and self-mocking at the same time" *Time Out*, New York

"The French have already called [Mabanckou] a young writer to watch. After this debut, I certainly concur" *Globe and Mail*, Toronto

"Broken Glass proves to be an obsessive, slyly playful raconteur . . . the prose runs wild to weave endless sentences, their rhythm and pace attuned to the narrator's rhetorical extravagances . . . With his sourly comic recollections, Broken Glass makes a fine companion" Peter Carty, *Independent*

"A book of grubby erudition . . . full of tall tales that can entertain readers from Brazzaville to Bognor" James Smart, *Guardian*

"Mabanckou's narrative gains an uplifting momentum of its own" Emma Hagestadt, *Independent*

"Mabanckou's irreverent wit and madcap energy have made him a big name in France . . . surreal" Giles Foden, *Condé Nast Traveller*

"Magical realism meets black comedy in an excellent satire by an inventive and playful writer" Alastair Mabbott, *Herald*

"Africa's Samuel Beckett . . . Mabanckou's freewheeling prose marries classical French elegance with Paris slang and a Congolese beat. It weds the oral culture of his mother to an omnivorous bibliophilia encouraged by his stepfather . . . *Memoirs of a Porcupine* draws on oral lore and parables in its sly critique of those who use traditional beliefs as a pretext for violence" *The Economist*

# BLACK BAZAAR

## ALAIN MABANCKOU

Translated by Sarah Ardizzone

A complete catalogue record for this book can be
obtained from the British Library on request

The right of Alain Mabanckou to be identified as the
author of this work has been asserted in accordance with
the Copyright, Designs and Patents Act 1988

First published as *Black Bazar* in 2009 by Éditions du Seuil, Paris
First published in this English translation in 2012 by Serpent's Tail,
an imprint of Profile Books Ltd
29 Cloth Fair
London EC1A 7JQ
*www.serpentstail.com*

ISBN 978 1 84668 777 8
eISBN 978 1 84765 657 5

Designed and typeset by Crow Books

To Pauline Kengué, my mother

# Prologue

Four months have come and gone since my partner ran off with our daughter and the Hybrid, this African drummer in a group nobody's ever heard of in France, and that's including in Corsica and Monaco. I'm trying to move out of this place, you see. I've had all I can take of my neighbour, Mr Hippocratic, he's always giving me a hard time, he spies on me when I take the rubbish down to the basement and he lays the blame for all the evils on earth at my door. And another thing, I keep thinking I can make out the figures of my ex and the Hybrid stalking me at home. It's not like I haven't cleaned the studio from top to bottom, or painted the walls yellow instead of the sky blue that was there before. So there's nothing left to remind me that a woman and child used to live here too. Except for the shoe that my partner must have forgotten in her rush. I guess she was worrying I might be back at any moment that day and that I'd catch her packing when I was just enjoying my Pelfort over at Jip's. Finding that shoe was partly thanks to a tip-off from one of my pals at Jip's, Paul from the big Congo. He'd confided in me over a couple of beers that when a woman leaves you've absolutely got to move your bed in order to draw a line under your past life and steer clear of nightmares involving small men who will haunt you and curse you. He was right. Sure enough, for seven nights after my ex left I had plenty of nightmares. I jumped off the Great Wall of China into thin air. I had wings, I could soar so high, I flew more than ten thousand kilometres in a few seconds, then I landed on a mountain peak ten times higher than the Himalayas and twenty-five times higher than our mountains in the Mayombe Forest. The pygmies of Gabon were circling me with their poisoned assegais. I couldn't shake them off, they were flying faster than me. When I was a boy, people used to claim those pygmies had supernatural powers because they were the first people entrusted by God with the keys of the earth since the time of Genesis. It was to them that the Lord dedicated the fifth day of Creation when he said: "Be fruitful and multiply and fill the earth . . ." At that time, the small men were still wondering what they would be able to eat down here, so God, who could read the thoughts of every creature, reassured our pygmies of Gabon by adding: "I give you every seed-bearing plant on the face of the whole earth, and every tree that has fruit with seed in it. They will be yours for food." These days, mankind destroys the flora and perhaps that's why the pygmies of Gabon come back to terrify us in our dreams.

During those nightmares, I would toss and turn in bed and sweat like I had a fever. The pygmies of Gabon were getting ready to hurl my daughter into a pot of boiling palm oil.

I called out:

"Oh no, boys, oh no you don't! That's my daughter! My daughter! My little Henriette! She's innocent. You can take me instead, if you like. But don't go putting humanity to shame, when you are our ancestors. Show the whole world that cannibalism doesn't exist where you come from, that it was invented by explorers, above all by those Africans who write books!"

And the oldest of them came towards me with his grey beard, his red eyes and his yellow teeth:

"Who told you we were cannibals, eh? We're vegetarians, one hundred per cent! We're only sacrificing your child so that the rains will come. We need all her blood, then we'll hand her back to you . . ."

I called out to my ex for help, and that's when I woke up with a jolt to realise there weren't any pygmies of Gabon, I was alone, and I'd fallen asleep without switching off the lights or the television.

It wasn't until I moved my bed that those small men finally disappeared . . .

* * *

I'm a regular at Jip's, the Afro-Cuban bar near the fountain at Les Halles in the 1st arrondissement, and these days you could say I'm even more of a regular than usual. Sometimes I doze off until I get woken by

the sound of chairs being stacked by Lazio the security
guard, who's cursing under his breath because someone
did a runner and he's the one who takes the rap, when
it's his job to sort out the riff-raff from the banlieues not
to worry about who has or hasn't settled their bill. Willy
the barman tells him there's no difference between a
thug who smashes the joint and a customer who hasn't
paid their bill. They've both got it coming, even if you
pull your punches with the non-payer . . .

Before walking into the bar, I always glance across to
where Soul Fashion, a ladies' underwear shop, used to
be. There's a reason for me looking that way: it's where
my ex used to work. The shop closed down and nobody
knows why. So now the Chinese guy with a restaurant
a bit further along, on Rue de la Grande Truanderie, is
opening a dry cleaners on the premises . . .

Lately, when I show up at Jip's, Roger the French-
Ivorian pounces on me. He's heard it from Paul from the
big Congo that, in order to drown my sorrows after my
ex left me and to control my anger against the Hybrid,
I'm writing a diary at home with a typewriter I bought
from a second-hand shop in Porte de Vincennes.

Take the day before yesterday, when he saw me
coming he didn't even give me time to reach the spot by
the bar where Paul from the big Congo often stands to
get a better view of the girls going by in Rue Saint-Denis.

He said to me:

"Here you are, Buttologist, just the person I've been

waiting for! Paul from the big Congo tells me you're writing this and that and it is called *Black Bazaar*. So what's your little scam? Why are you writing? I suppose you think anyone can write stories, eh? Is this a trick to claim that you are unemployed, to squeeze through the chinks in the system, to steal other people's benefits, to dig an even deeper hole in the social security and to put the brakes on Gallic social mobility?"

Roger the French-Ivorian understood that I didn't appreciate his tone of voice and ordered two Pelforts to win me back.

"Listen, my friend, you must be realistic here! Forget about sitting down and writing every day, there are much smarter people for that, and you can see them on the telly, they know how to talk, and when they talk there is a subject, there is a verb and there is an object. This is what they were born to do, they were brought up with it, but when it comes to us negroes, well then writing is not our thing. With us it is the oral traditions of our ancestors, we are tales from the bush and forest, the adventures of Leuk-the-Hare told to children around a fire crackling to the beat of the tom-tom. Our problem it is that we did not invent the printing press or the ballpoint pen, and we will always sit at the back of the classroom fantasising about how to write the history of the dark continent with our spears. Do you understand what I am saying? Plus we have got a funny accent, you can hear it even when we write, and this people do not like. And another thing, you need real life experience to write. What real life experience have you got, eh? Nothing! Zero! Now take me, I would have no end of things to write about because I am mixed-race, I am lighter-skinned than you are, and this gives me an important edge. My only reason for not writing a single line until now is lack of time. But I will make up for it when I am retired with a nice house in the countryside, and the whole world will recognise my work for the masterpiece that it is!"

He downed his glass of Pelfort in one and then, after a moment's silence, he asked:

"Since you say you are a writer, have you at least got a white sheep in these stories of yours?"

I told Roger the French-Ivorian I didn't like sheep and that I had never seen any that colour.

"You mean there aren't any sheep in your district, over there in the Congo?"

"Well yes, you will find some among the traders in Trois-Cents, but their sheep aren't even white, they are all black, with patches sometimes, and you can't go telling credible stories with sheep like that. And another thing, the traders chop them up and sell them as kebabs at night in the streets."

"Fine, all right then, but in these stories of yours, have you at least got a sea and an old man who goes fishing with a young boy?"

I said no because the sea frightens me especially since,

like a lot of people in our country, I went to see *Jaws* and had to leave The Rex before the end of the film.

Roger the French-Ivorian signalled to Willy for two more Pelforts.

"Fine, all right then," he went on, "but in these stories of yours, have you at least got an old man who reads love stories in the middle of the bush?"

"Oh no, and anyway how would we get love stories to the heart of the bush? Back home it would be mission impossible, our interior is closed off. There is only one road that goes there, and it dates back to colonial times."

"You have been independent for nearly half a century and you're telling me there's only one road? What the hell have you been doing in all that time? You've got to stop blaming those settlers for everything! The Whites cleared off and they left you everything including colonial homes, electricity, a railway, drinking water, a river, an Atlantic Ocean, a seaport, Nivaquine, antiseptic and a town centre!"

"It's nothing to do with me, it's our governments who are to blame. If they had at least resurfaced the road the settlers left us, then today your old man could be sent his love stories. But let me tell you, that colonial road is a scandal . . ."

"What is the matter, eh? Why is it a scandal? Are you against the settlers or what? I say we owe the settlers respect! Me, I've had enough of people talking through their hats when those settlers conscientiously got on with their job of delivering us from the darkness and bringing us civilisation. Did they have to do all that, eh? You do realise that they worked like lunatics? There were mosquitoes, devils, sorcerers, cannibals and green mambas, there was sleeping sickness, yellow fever, blue fever, orange fever, rainbow fever and goodness knows what else. There were all these ills over our ebony lands, our ghostly Africa, to the point that even Tintin ended up having to come over in person on our behalf. So far be it from me to harbour a grudge against the settlers. You do accept that Tintin went to your Congo, don't you? And did that Tintin ask himself a thousand and one questions? Didn't he come with his friends, a captain with a beard who insults everybody and a small dog with more intelligence than you or I put together, eh? And if he managed to get there, well then, in these stories of yours, you can include some love stories to that old man along the colonial road!"

"Yes, but that road's too dangerous, especially during the rains."

"What's the problem?"

"It never stops raining back home, and when it rains it is a thousand times worse than the Flood . . ."

After one round of silence and two gulps of beer, Roger the French-Ivorian, annoyed that I've always got an answer for everything, slammed his fist down on the table:

"I'm just trying to help you out here! Writing's no joke, you do understand that, eh? It's up to the people who the write stories to invent situations, not me. So fire up your imagination, help that old man who's bored rigid out there in the bush to get hold of some love stories!"

When I didn't answer, he capitulated:

"Fine, all right then, I'm getting worked up for nothing, I'm sorry, perhaps I'm asking you something impossible. The thing is, I'm trying to work out how difficult this is. But in these stories of yours, have you at least got a young Japanese compulsive liar who tells her analyst she can't hear music any more, by which I mean she can no longer experience pleasure?"

It was my turn to get annoyed:

"Oh no, oh no you don't, I'm not going all the way to Japan for a story about a compulsive liar who can't get her kicks!"

"Have you got it in for the Japanese, or what?"

"Not at all, but why not go to Haiti too while we're at it, and talk about voodoo, eh? What's got into you? Are you some kind of sex maniac? Have you ever pleasured a woman?"

"Shhh! There's no need to shout like that and insult me, everyone can hear you in the bar, and that won't do. A writer should be discreet, he should observe his surroundings so he can describe them in minute detail . . . But in these stories of yours, have you at least got a drunkard who goes to the land of the dead to find his palm wine supplier who accidentally died at the foot of a palm tree?"

I said no because I've never set foot in the land of the dead and have no intention of doing so, not for anything in the world, especially since it's even further away than Japan and Haiti.

"Yes, but you're only telling a story, so just imagine you're going there. That's not so difficult, is it?"

"I won't go there. Some places are asking for trouble, and stories about people who go to the land of the dead are not my kind of thing."

"Fine, all right then, but in these stories of yours have you at least got a great love that takes place in the time of cholera between a poor telegrapher and a young schoolgirl who will end up marrying a doctor later on?"

"What is a telegrapher?" I asked, playing innocent.

"I can see we're not out of the woods yet! We're going to have to work on your vocabulary . . . But in these stories of yours, have you at least got a crime of passion involving an artist who murders a woman he met at an exhibition, even though she admired one of his paintings?"

"Don't talk to me about art!"

"Really? You don't like art but you call yourself a writer?"

"Modern art gets up my nose. Back home, I saw a reproduction of a painting at the French Cultural Centre, it was called *Les Demoiselles d'Avignon*, and it was ugly as a bulldog's face."

"So you don't understand the first thing about

painting, which is a major handicap . . . But in these stories of yours, have you at least got a character with a drum, somebody who from the age of three doesn't want to grow up, a character who will be interned in a mental hospital later on and who will tell their life story to their keeper through the peep-hole, eh? Now, I'm only saying all this to help you out a bit because you don't have a clue where you are going or who else has gone before you. It would help if the keeper in the mental hospital had an artistic streak, he might tie knots, for example, which he would show to the patient, do you see where I'm going, eh?"

I let it drop that I've got a character who plays the tom-toms, and that I've nicknamed him the Hybrid. He's the guy who's gone back to the home country with my partner and my daughter.

"Mention drums or tom-toms again and I'm walking out of this bar!" I bellowed. "I've had enough! I'm off!"

And I made a swift exit from Jip's, because Roger the French-Ivorian was getting more and more drunk. I told him I'd never talk to him about any of my projects again, and that he'd be better off forgetting what Paul from the big Congo had said to him.

My parting shot was:

"You don't understand anything. I write the way I lead my life, one moment it's one thing and the next I've moved on to a whole different kettle of fish, and that's called living too in case you didn't know. Buying me a few Pelforts doesn't give you the right to shit all over me with your white sheep and your old men who like going to sea and reading love stories. I've got a real friend who listens to me, he's called Louis-Philippe and he's from Haiti. Now that's what I call a writer, not some loudmouth like you waiting to retire before you produce your masterpiece for all the world to read. Go and find someone else to pick on!"

Just as Paul from the big Congo walked in, I heard Roger the French-Ivorian answer in a metallic voice:

"Down here, Buttologist, everything has already been written! Everything! Take it from me, I've read all the great books in the world. So don't go thinking you can change things. And you'd better make sure I don't find my name in your diary of a cuckold! Speaking of which, where are your woman and daughter now, eh? You can't put that into writing because you're ashamed of people finding out. Call yourself a writer? You're just vomiting up your anger against your ex and the minstrel who stole her off you. Serves you right!"

It's definitely not me who's digging the hole in the social security. It was already around when I got here, everybody had been talking about it for decades. Some people even claimed you could fall into it just from walking in the street, because there were no warning signs, so I had nothing to be ashamed of and, to boost my morale, I kept telling myself this hole story was made up by a few opposition politicians who wanted to stop the government from doing its work so it would have a disastrous track record when it came to the elections . . .

But the people debating it on telly a week ago declared that at this rate we were heading straight for "a spectacular and unprecedented collapse". They've got me feeling very worried again, especially since even Roger the French-Ivorian is making it clear he thinks I am personally making matters worse by only working part-time and spending the rest of my time in front of my typewriter . . .

From listening to those well-informed people on the telly talking about it, I was led to believe that the situation was worse than serious, it was hopeless. The country had lost the battle and the war. They talked about the deficit, about bad management, about calamitous governance and lots of other things too. I scribbled notes on the labels off the Pelfort bottles I'd bought the day before from our Arab on the corner, who's very friendly and always starts talking as soon as I walk in:

"'For too long the West has force-fed us with lies and bloated us with pestilence' . . . Do you know which black poet had the courage to say that, eh?"

I couldn't take my eyes off the screen during that heated debate. Which was an achievement for me. I generally prefer to watch romantic movies or shows that promise me a chance of winning an automatic car if I dial the telephone number at the bottom of the screen. Oh, and I used to like watching those shows with couples who get catapulted to an island in South America where they're separated and exposed to the temptations of other men and women twenty-four seven, for twelve days. It's true, back then I never missed an episode, I used to joke with my ex and dare her to set off with me on one of those adventures, because apparently it's when they're far away from home that couples realise how unshakeable their love is. You'd keep watching to find out whether the man and the woman would head back home together, arm in arm at the end, or whether they'd be calling each other every name under the sun and never speak again. My partner didn't find it funny when I suggested going for it, she was convinced I was just dreaming of getting down and dirty with all those blondes, redheads and brunettes with nice curvy backsides like the women from back home, the ones I go wild for. She said that the women we saw on telly weren't real, it was all down to the make-up, because she'd never met a woman who looked anything like that when she was out shopping in Franprix or Monoprix at the end of our street. She also gave me a hard time because some of the men and women who were stranded on the island gave into the sins of the flesh from day one, and you could see them fornicating in the pool; while others observed a brief period of abstinence before making up for lost time and doing the business in every grove of that paradise. Now according to her, I belonged to the first category of sinners who were in a hurry to take a bite out of the first apple that landed in their lap. It's been a while since I stopped watching those kinds of shows, because I found out they've often got fake couples leading viewers up the tropical garden path. Is that any way to go about things . . . ?

So this time I was watching something else, a debate that was indirectly laying the blame at my door. Up on stage, a fight was about to break out among the guests. They said the words "hole" and "social security" nine hundred and twenty-five times. We watched a report from a health insurance office and one from a chemist. As chance would have it, the reports had been filmed in our neighbourhood, a bit further off, towards the town hall. The men and women featured were openly criticising our social security system, they didn't realise the place was bugged with tiny microphones and cameras, or that they'd be watched throughout France, including in Corsica and Monaco. They were explaining how they often turned a blind eye to false claims because they couldn't give a monkey's, and anyway the money that got squandered in reimbursements for this or that didn't come out of their own pockets . . .

We needed answers at the end of the programme, but all we got were generalisations. "The State must play its part," boomed a bald guy, pulling his last two remaining hairs up from his neck and down over his jutting forehead. "Urgent times call for drastic measures", said a badly shaven guest, who had probably been using his wife's hair-removal cream. "We need a Marshall Plan hic et nunc" proffered a man who, to camera and in profile, looked like a sole. "We need to tighten our belts", added a woman wearing glasses with lenses thick as bicycle wheels from the early years of the Occupation. "We need . . . we need, we need to look at . . . to look at . . . the behaviour of . . . of those on so . . . so . . . social . . . benefits, git . . . git . . . get . . . them to change their habits and useless . . . get them

to use less medishit . . . shit . . . medicine. And we also
. . . we also . . . need to organise a crackdown on fraud",
was the response of a man who stammered from the
off and had trouble finishing his sentences. The theme
music started up, the debaters smiled and congratulated
themselves, pleased at putting in a good performance.

I knew my neighbour had been watching the same
programme. I could hear his telly from my studio.
What I didn't know was how much of a pain in the
neck he was going to be about this story . . .

* * *

The next day, when I was still red-eyed from watching
that spat on the telly, my neighbour from across the
hallway ran into me down by the bins and accosted me
in a sarcastic tone of voice:

"You hardly need me to tell you, this situation is
serious! Very serious! They're saying the hole in the
social security is getting deeper and deeper because
there's riff-raff out there, with no sense of republican
values, threatening our democracy. Now, I'm naming
no names here, but something has got to be done!"

Why was he saying this to me? We don't get on, the
two of us. We barely speak, and there's never been a
good feeling since the day I set foot in this building
with my suitcases of clothes to live with the woman
who would later become the mother of my daughter.

I took my time before answering, I didn't want to

lose my temper. I told him that I understood what he was talking about, that I had watched the programme too. And that yes, the hole in the social certainly was deep and there were already plenty of victims who had fallen into it. That I'd been asking myself a thousand and one questions since that debate. And that I wanted to get a clearer picture of what was going on.

"Yes, but something needs doing right now! Enough is enough, I've had it with people like you who are always waiting to get a clearer picture, and all the time that hole just keeps growing. Tell me, while we're on the subject, is it your new vocation to stay at home and type every day on a goddam typewriter that makes the whole building shake? Does that really put bread on the table or is it because you don't want to admit to people that you're unemployed?"

Having failed to get a rise out of me he paused, before leaving the basement, to examine my shoes and my Cerutti 1884 suit. I was convinced I must have trodden in something or that there were dirty marks on my clothes.

"When you're taking your rubbish down to the bins, is it really necessary to dress up like a dandy going to a wedding, eh?" he rattled off, sounding vexed. "Those clothes must have cost a king's ransom!"

I don't know what makes him think I buy my clothes using state benefits, in other words his money. He's the one who is popping pills all day long, stocking up again when the fancy takes him, getting various doctors to make home visits. The fact of the matter is he's become more and more insufferable since his accident on the fifth floor. If he'd been happy to cultivate his own garden, nothing would have happened to him. But his problem is that he spends all his time going up and down the stairwell, spying on the residents' every move, finding out what people get up to in their own homes, keeping tabs on their comings and goings in the corridors.

It's two months ago now since he fell and hit his head, and I can still remember how everybody in the building was scared that day because a nice fellow from the second floor who watches a lot of detective films explained to us how an inspector would lead a lengthy police investigation, that we would be on the evening news on the telly, and that people would see us in flesh and blood across all of France, including in Corsica and Monaco . . .

And I remember how, when the neighbour slipped on the stairs, I stopped writing and opened my door because from the screeching up there you'd have thought a wild boar was having its throat slit with a chainsaw like something straight out of *Scarface*. We could hear him going thud on each step like a sack of potatoes, from the fifth floor all the way down to the ground floor where I was. He blacked out in front of my door, arms splayed. The tenants came rushing down, some of them barefoot, others with towels wrapped round their waists. We could see he was dead for good, so we decided we'd better call the emergency services. But someone from the sixth floor, who knew what to do in situations like that, announced it wasn't an ambulance we needed but an undertaker or a pathologist. He warned us that the emergency services these days wouldn't stand for being messed around, they'd had enough of being called out for nursery school bumps and bruises every thirty seconds, and now their union was threatening to make people pay for crazy call-outs.

"The person who rings pays the call-out fee, not me!" he emphasised.

So we dropped the idea, but the corpse was still there, in front of us. The nice fellow from the second floor who watches too many detective films warned us that we would soon get a visit from someone cantankerous, a German cousin of Inspector Colombo, that he would wear a raincoat and drive an old banger which he'd park in front of our building, that he'd smoke a smelly cigar, that he'd talk to us about his wife and his dog, that he'd pretend not to notice anything, that he'd lay traps for us, that he'd tire us out with his questions about this, that and the other, that he'd look for clues on the soles of our shoes, on our cigarette stubs, our beer glasses, our dusty doormats, in our condoms and our jacket pockets, in lipsticks, on badly knotted ties, on our grubby front door knobs, down by the bins, that

---

he'd have a word with the Arab on the corner, then with the Chinese, then with the Pakistanis, then with the Indians, then with the Greeks, then with the Polish plumbers, that he'd take fingerprint samples from every landing, that he'd want to know what we'd been up to before the drama took place, what we ate two days before, what we drank a month before, that he'd look into what relations were like between the residents, that he'd spend time down in the basements, that he'd pay close attention to all the numbers we had dialled – even Freefone numbers – that he'd also take his time over the calls we had received, even if it was just someone trying to sell us a second-hand vacuum cleaner or to make us switch telephone suppliers. Not only that, but Colombo's cousin would summon everyone who had paid us a visit over the last twenty and a half years minimum. And after all that, some of us would still have to spend hours in custody, in a police station with a stuttering lawyer appointed by the court, and officers who would treat the suspects like guinea pigs for new torture methods from the United States that are used to worm information fast out of people who try it on during the interrogation sessions.

"Get your alibis ready, and make a note of them one by one on a piece of paper," he advised us.

At this point, a man who lives on the seventh floor, Staircase A, brought it to our attention that he could be ruled out for a start, none of this had anything to do with him, he had what is called a "cast iron alibi": he'd been away for a month, he had only got back two hours before the accident, he'd been in the Dordogne staying in Champagnac-de-Belair with his mother, who had been suffering from cancer for years.

"And anyway I live on Staircase A, whereas the incident happened on Staircase B, so it's clearly got nothing to do with me. If Colombo's German cousin so much as sets foot in this building to hassle me, I swear I'm filing a complaint, I'm hiring Jacques Vergès as my lawyer and I'm passing the details on to the relevant human rights bodies in this country!"

The nice fellow who watches the detective films pointed out that Colombo's German cousin would drive all the way to Champagnac-de-Belair in his old banger and that he wouldn't give a monkey's whether it was Staircase A or B, that he would summon the sick mother in question, cancer or no cancer, because in criminal law sickness is no excuse for murder and vice versa, and that in any event there would be all sorts of upheaval in our building. His conclusion was that we shouldn't touch the corpse, the investigation would take at least two to three and a half years to establish the cause of the fall and if some of us were implicated in this story . . .

All the same, we stood there staring at the corpse because it isn't every day you get to examine a fresh stiff in your own building instead of in those films where people lie to us and take us for kids by pretending to be dead when you can see they're breathing, and the blood on them is that ketchup they sell at La Chapelle market.

We surrounded the corpse and were still figuring out what to do when the man who lives on the first floor reminded us:

"Look here, he's stopped breathing!"

"He's not a pretty sight, we should cover him up quickly with a white sheet," added the man just back from Champagnac-de-Belair.

"He's peed his pants, and there's dribble coming out of his mouth," said the man from the third floor, going one further.

"That's weird, can you see how he's got one eye bigger than the other now?" chipped in a woman from the fourth floor.

"Don't touch him! Don't touch him!" bellowed the man who watches the detective films.

And that's when the neighbour suddenly woke up with a jolt and roared at us:

"I'm not dead! I'm not dead!"

We shrank back because he looked like a ghost in a horror film, *Night of the Living Dead* for example.

"Who just said I've got one eye bigger than the other, eh? Was it that slut from the fourth floor? Don't you dare lay a finger on me, you bastards! Someone pushed me, and you're all in it together! You're going to hear me out!"

He had blood on his face, he had several battered ribs, and he was grimacing with the pain. We tried to get close to help him stand up.

"Don't touch me, you murderers! Someone left a banana skin on the stairs, and he's going to hear me out! I know who did it!"

We all looked at each other and raised our hands in the air, as if a firearm was being trained on us, to show we had nothing to do with this banana skin story. Then the neighbour barricaded himself in his apartment and spent the day phoning every doctor in town and raining down insults on them, because they didn't understand how a normal person could fall from the fifth floor to the ground floor without someone pushing them.

The neighbour wouldn't stop snorting and muttering to himself:

"Goddammit! I'm telling you an African laid a trap for me with a banana skin! And we're not talking any old banana skin! That banana came directly from Africa!"

The thing I wanted to know was what on earth was he doing up on the fifth floor, when he lives on the ground floor like me. Anyway, that's why he's got a bandage on his head now and spends his days sniffing at a little bottle . . .

*  *  *

Unluckily for me, my studio is slap bang next to the neighbour's apartment. I can hear him cackling like a hyena in front of his telly and bellowing into the phone when the doctor on the other end of the line explains he won't be able to pay him a home visit. The neighbour reminds the doctor about the Hippocratic Oath and promises to get him struck off professionally:

"Don't betray the Hippocratic Oath! You swore that oath, Doctor! You promised to treat the poor and needy and whosoever seeks your help!"

Because he keeps going on about the Hippocratic Oath, we've ended up nicknaming him Mr Hippocratic. Seeing as he can't insult the whole earth, he takes it out on me instead. Mr Hippocratic likes to cultivate his garden at my expense. He says, for example, that like most Blacks he knows, I always put the cart before the horse, I'm not worth peanuts, I'm a cabbage head, with an artichoke for a heart, I don't have a bean to my name, I'm knee-high to a grasshopper, and pea-brained to boot, I lead people up the garden path, I might think I'm the biggest pumpkin on the patch but I'll be pushing up the daisies like the rest of them . . .

When his anger gets the better of him he pounds on the wall, complaining there are too many visitors coming by my place, that I'm the one who's digging the hole in the social, that my studio is turning into Château Rouge market, into the headquarters of the African underworld, that nobody has any idea what we're getting up to inside, that for all he knows we're holding man-on-man orgies – that there may even be wild animals involved – that we're printing fake money, that we're smoking the devil's lettuce or the wacky baccy, that we're illegally dealing I don't know what new drug, that we're running riot in "his building" which used to be a calm and pleasant block to live in before the mass influx of the Senegalese soldiers together with the natives of the Republic. He says the settlers didn't finish off their job properly, that he'll always hold this against them, that they should have whipped us harder in order to drum good manners into us. That the trouble with those French colonisers was never seeing things all the way through . . .

*   *   *

Mr Hippocratic is only a tenant, but from the way he behaves you'd think he owned the place. People mistake him for the caretaker because his apartment is just by the main entrance and the postman has been known to leave parcels and recorded delivery letters for other residents in front of his door. The poor tenants in question have to track these down to the bins in the basement.

I couldn't tell you how he's managed to find out that I'm a month in arrears with the rent or that I haven't taken out household insurance with his insurer at the end of the road. Not to mention the noises and smells he claims get produced by me and my friends when we're cooking our food and listening to our music from back home, so as to forget our everyday worries for a while. He doesn't know the first thing about nostalgia. France is his country, and he boasts to me about how proud he is to be French by birth. I've heard him complaining, for example, that France can no longer shelter all the destitute in the world, especially the Congolese who are forever turning up at the border even though they've got oil and aphrodisiacs like bois bandé back home. There are other countries in Europe, so why don't we go and live there instead, or else head back to our huts of beaten earth. And he spouts this drivel while staring defiantly at me. One time, when he got a bit tipsy, I convinced myself he was going to slit my throat down by the bins. But he'd only laid into the booze so he could bring up everything he'd been harbouring a grudge about for ages.

Sometimes I feel like smashing his face in, but what's the point when the stairs can take care of it? I don't want any trouble. You get people like that, you see them, you think they're healthy enough, you shake them up a bit, and the next thing you know you've laid yourself wide open to trouble because all it takes is for them to bash into a wall on purpose – even if it's only made of plywood – and they'll start claiming assault and grievous bodily harm leading directly to them snuffing it.

So I don't take any notice when he's trying to get a rise out of me. But he's always on my case. He's after confrontation. He steals my doormats and dumps rotten fruit in front of my door. I know it's him, and nobody but him, I don't see who else in this block would act that way. I don't have any problems with the other tenants . . .

* * *

Mr Hippocratic has had it in for me from the day I moved into this studio. One evening, my ex had told me not to forget to take the rubbish out, so I went down to the basement with a torch. I could feel someone breathing behind me. Someone padding along. I turned around and who should I see but Mr Hippocratic.

"So your country is the Congo, isn't it?" he asked, without telling me how he knew.

"Yes," I replied.

"Did you see the telly last night?"

"No, I was busy, I didn't watch TV . . ."

"Dearie me, the poor Congolese, we've got to do something for them! There are diseases, there is famine, they have many wives, and they are always fighting all the time, poor things! And the president of these Congolese I'm talking about, what's his name again?"

"Denis Sassou Nguesso . . ."

"Oh no, that's not it, that's not the name I heard on the telly! That's not the name at all! It was a longer name, more of an African name, by which I mean rather barbarian sounding . . ."

"Mobutu Sese Seko Nkuku Ngbendu wa za Banga?"

"Yes! Yes! Yes! That's the name! Something has got to be done, the poor Congolese are all going to die of starvation or AIDS or because of tribal wars . . ."

"That President Mobutu is already dead, you must have seen a programme about former Zaire and the regime that Mobutu . . ."

"Oh no he's not, Mobutu's not dead! I saw him on telly last night with my own eyes! He's your president, and he was in the pink of health! He was giving a speech in a packed stadium. Apparently it was in the same stadium where he murdered and buried Patrice Lumumba. That Mobutu makes his people suffer, he is a villain, he is evil, he's a dictator, we should send in the Americans to do a spot of mopping up over there! That man brings shame on your race, it's intolerable! If I were an African I would rise up, I'd go and fight against that dictator. Hasn't he ever heard of democracy, that president of yours? He sells your diamonds, he buys himself fancy homes in Europe, is that a normal way to behave?"

When I didn't react, Mr Hippocratic started up again:

"And what about you, as a Congolese man living like a coward in Europe, what are you actually doing for your poor country where there are diseases, where there is famine, where the men have many wives at the same time and on top of that they are always fighting, eh?"

"I'm from the other Congo, the small Congo, Congo-Brazzaville. There's another Congo which is bigger and where . . . "

"No, it was definitely your country on the telly yesterday, with that president with the long name who wears glasses and a leopard-skin hat. He walks with a stick! Are you telling me you don't know who your own president is? I find that shocking! I'm telling you I saw him with my own eyes on the telly . . . !"

\* \* \*

Even when my partner and our daughter were still living here, Mr Hippocratic would already be snooping on us through his spy-hole at the first sign of noise in the corridor. I know this because I could hear him tiptoeing over to his door and holding his froggy breath. And when our daughter was born, he wanted to know if I had triplets and not just one baby because a single child couldn't possibly bawl fit for an entire nursery school. And off he went to snivel at our landlord about how there were small groups of Africans who were stirring up ill-feeling in the block, who were turning the premises into a tropical capital, who slit the throats of cockerels at five in the morning to collect their blood, who beat the tom-toms all night long to send coded messages to their bush spirits and put a jinx on France. That they should be sent back home, or he'd refuse to pay his rent and taxes any more, he'd go and give evidence at the local police station, and these immigrants would be allocated a one-way ticket on a charter flight, even if it was the French taxpayer who had to pick up the tab for their return to the native land.

I let him have his way. I've got nothing to add to his wild rants because back in the home country we were always taught to respect our elders, especially when they've got grey hair, which is the case for Mr Hippocratic. Each time I tell him I agree with him, that if negroes have wide noses it's simply so they can wear glasses, and that the black man does not live by bread alone but also by sweet potatoes and plantains.

And since I'm not the type to pick a quarrel with anybody, I've decided the only answer is to move out. Unlike my ex who didn't like the banlieue, I'm willing to go and live there, but I don't want to move back into that studio in Château d'Eau I used to share with several of my compatriots. In life, you should never go back to square one.

I've visited a lot of studios in the area. Nothing doing. I'd need decent payslips, but I've been working part-time since my ex left, so I don't see how I'll ever leave this place.

I don't talk to Mr Hippocratic any more. I try to make sure I come home when he's already asleep. And when we cross paths in the hallway or down by the bins, we stare at each other defiantly. He spits on the ground and shouts:

"Bloody Congolese! Your woman's walked out on you! Go back to where you come from!"

Now, if I were a nasty piece of work like him, I'd have evened the score a long time ago:

"Bloody Martiniquais! Go back to your island in the Caribbean!"

When I check out my profile in the mirror, I reckon I'm not a bad-looking guy. I wouldn't even begin to compare myself with that minstrel who's gone off with my ex and taken my daughter with them. Between him and me it's like night and day. I'm tall and nicely proportioned; he's such a midget you don't even notice him when he walks past. If you're not careful you might trample him underfoot or mistake him for a four-legged animal with no tail. I've got a small moustache and I'm handsome; he looks like a primate who narrowly missed out on evolving into a human. So that nickname of the Hybrid I gave him fits like a glove. As for the way he dresses, it's a disaster! Does being an artist mean he's got to wear threads like that? What a load of bull, I know artists who are always snappily dressed with shades and a fan for flaunting it. When it comes to clothes I don't mess around, and my friends at Jip's understand this, including Roger the French-Ivorian. I'm not trying to show off, but my suits are tailor-made. I buy them in Italy, in Bologna to be precise, where I scour the shops, stopping at each boutique in the city's arcades. When I moved in here I didn't know where to store it all. I've got six big suitcases of clothes and shoes – mostly crocodile, anaconda and lizard-skin Westons, as well as Church's, Bowens and some other English shoes.

I make a point of wearing a suit because you've got to "keep up appearances", as we say among the Society for Ambient People and Persons of Elegance, SAPPE, which, without wanting to be contentious, is an invention from back home, born in the Bacongo district of Brazzaville, towards the Total roundabout. We're the ones who exported "Sappe" to Paris, and don't let anyone tell you otherwise, because lately there are so many false prophets swarming these streets in the City of Light, to the point where it's getting difficult to separate the wheat from the chaff.

Of course, some people will argue that the Ivorians and the Cameroonians are Sappers too. Well let's just see about that, shall we, they only started making an effort, poor things, because they complained their women were after us. So they thought it was down to our Westons and our Gianni Versace jackets. But when these desperate Ivorians or distraught Cameroonians wear the same clothes as us, there's no competition, we're talking night and day; the Congolese Sapper wins out every time thanks to his inimitable style, and that's not me being biased here, it's just the harsh reality, and I'd be lying if I said any different . . .

Linen jackets by Emmanuel Ungaro that crease elegantly

and are worn with refinement. Terylene jackets by Francesco Smalto. One hundred per cent or even two hundred per cent lambswool jackets in pure Cerruti 1884 fabric. Jacquard socks. Silk ties, including motifs of the Eiffel Tower or the Arc de Triomphe. That's my style. And just some of what I've got in my suitcases . . .

I'm fanatical about Italian collars with three or four buttons, I like to feel them around my neck, stiff, folded double, uncreasable. Tell me how you knot your tie and I will tell you who you are – and even what company you keep. The people who go on telly don't have a clue. They buy their ties from the first shop they walk into and then have the nerve to splash their face across all of France, including in Corsica and Monaco. It shouldn't be allowed. When I'm watching a panel discussion on telly, like last time, I can tell how the participants are going to behave just by spotting their tie.

When I'm outside Jip's, I've been known to feel sorry for, to burst out laughing at, and even to fight the urge to go to the rescue of the idiot who has neglected this small detail that makes a world of difference.

Broadly speaking, I've noticed that shy men wear their ties tightly knotted, and in our crowd we call them suicidals. As for the thugs – who we call pimps – they look like men at the gallows with their knot close to the throat, while the show-offs plump theirs up big time. They deserve their nickname of cooking pot lids because they have this cast iron belief that the best is always on the outside and not on the inside.

The ones we dub bulls with no style are messy, their tie-knots look like the bony humps on an ass's back, and they don't even notice until the day their girlfriend points it out to them in despair.

The austere and meticulous ones – or priests in our language – do everything to make sure their tie doesn't move. They can spend a whole day without readjusting it. The chatterboxes – or sparrows – wear a loose knot.

The cuckolds – or has-beens – wear theirs to the side, sometimes it's even the wrong way round. Do I need to remind you I'm no cuckold, seeing as I wasn't married to my ex?

And last of all, the egoists, skinflints and whingers, otherwise known as the ants, don't change the knot until the tie has worn out. They never learnt how to tie their own knot, so they trust the sales assistant and never undo what was knotted for them in the shop, in front of the till.

And to think some evil spirits preach from their pinnacle of blindness that the habit does not the monk make! My eye! They haven't understood anything. The habit may not make the monk, but it's thanks to the habit we recognise him. And sometimes that habit causes us problems. This came home to me when I found myself being mistaken for somebody I wasn't. I felt so humiliated, I still haven't got over it.

I was at the Gare du Nord and I had to get to La Courneuve where my cousin was organising a party. Some movers and shakers from the Parisian nigger-trash had been invited and I knew that basically it was an excuse to parade the latest suits fashionable on the streets of Paris. When it's like that, we always turn up in sharp threads, well shaven and smelling fine, we stand there glaring at one another and casing the joint, we're checking to see if there are any new girls from back home worth hanging around for, because when these wild gazelles turn up in Paris with the dirt fresh on them you don't want to leave them any time to understand how the métro works or which counter they're supposed to go to for their family allowance. If you do, they'll go right ahead and dig an even deeper hole in the social for you. So you've got to grab hold of them fast, before they get the hang of things, ditch their country bumpkin accent to answer you in snooty tones and step out exclusively with small Whites who'll chuck them away afterwards like the Kleenexes sold by the Arab on the corner. It's a routine for us, but we like it like that, and the deal is never to go to one of these parties with your wife or girlfriend: you don't take a sandwich to a restaurant. You never know when you're going to take a shine to a nice plump gazelle fresh off the boat. It was a whole scene explaining to my ex that it would be better if she stayed at home. I told her she'd be bored out of her mind, that she'd be standing there staring into space, that nobody would talk to her because when you get a bunch of Congolese together in a corner, or even in a pocket handkerchief, they immediately start yelling in their own patois – and God knows we've got so many of these languages, you wonder how on earth we understand each other in our Tower of Babel. And then, seeing as my ex didn't drink alcohol, I used to point out that the people from back home are horrified by water, orange juice or any other fruit juice, and that drinking anything of the sort in front of them would be an insult. At which point she beat a retreat and gave me the green light . . .

So, on the day I'm talking about, I'd managed to convince her once again not to come with me. I'd spent the afternoon haggling with her. And I kept on checking my watch, which didn't help matters.

"Why are you in such a hurry, if it's only a gathering of Congolese talking in their patois?"

I kept pacing about our studio. I couldn't decide which suit to wear. I'd opened every suitcase and spread my clothes all over the floor as well as on the bed. In the end, I put on a bottle-green Yves Saint-Laurent suit with my burgundy Westons. Even our Arab on the corner stepped outside his shop when he smelled my aftershave. He waved at me from a distance, giving me the thumbs-up. I smiled at him, and walked down our street in the direction of the Chinese and Pakistani shops on my way to métro Marx Dormoy.

I could have caught a cab, but why miss out on the looks of passers-by? So I walked from Marx Dormoy as far as Porte de la Chapelle, and then on to the main entrance of the Gare du Nord.

It looked like a grand market where people were fighting over the final scraps on the eve of a world war breaking out. They were running everywhere. Some were staring hard at those screens with the train times on them. That's when I realised I was caught in the same trap as everybody else: there was a general transport strike on.

I elbowed my way to the platform. It was airless down there, but nobody wanted to leave because during a strike it's always when you decide to turn back that the train comes. You can't trust the timetables, and the guys from the RATP and the SNCF play with the passengers' nerves. They mutter incomprehensible messages into the loud speakers. They advise you to exit the station, to go back up to street level, to walk along Rue Magenta, then Rue Lafayette, then Rue de Strasbourg where, as if by magic, you'll find a bus that will tip you out like torture victims over towards the east of Paris, and too bad if you were heading west because the workers over that way have been up in arms for the past ten and a half years.

People wouldn't stop looking at me. Naturally, I assumed it was my suit, my shoes and my aftershave. So I adjusted my tie and straightened my trousers until

they fell neatly over my shoes. I undid three of my jacket
buttons, which is a special technique I have for showing
off my Christian Dior belt to its best advantage. And
then, all of a sudden, a man broke free from the crowd
like a rugby player hoping to score a try in a space as
narrow as a telephone box. He was filthy enough to
have stepped straight out of *The Dirty Havana Trilogy*
by Pedro Juan Guttiérrez, a novel I'd borrowed when
I was round at my friend's, the Haitian writer Louis-
Philippe, and which I'd been reading for a few days
now on public transport.

The man came up and shouted at me, point-blank:

"Hey, you, why are you on strike? Don't you
think you're going too far this time? You've got your
welfare benefits and the whole package, but you're
still ruining our lives! People complain there are
no more jobs in France, when the state has to keep
slackers, praying mantises and snails like you on its
payroll. Do you get your kicks out of taking people
hostage, eh? If you ask me, we should clean up the
SNCF and the RATP with bleach! Let's get rid of all
those idiots loitering in the street with their placards,
when they should be in the ticket office or at the
controls of their train. Right, now tell me what time
the next RER is due because these shitty screens have
stopped working too!"

I had no idea what was going on. Everyone was
shouting at me and agreeing with my assailant:

"Too right, let's get rid of the bastards! They're on strike twenty-nine days out of thirty!"

"Well said. I've had it up to here with these strikes!"

"Slackers, the lot of them!"

"Take early retirement. Make way for the young!"

"Why are you on the platform instead of finding us a train, eh?"

And seeing as I just stood there saying nothing, the original angry man disappeared into the crowd while calling me every revolting name under the sun that would have infuriated and outraged anyone who still has free time in their life to sing the praises of Negritude, but not me.

It took me a while to realise why they were laying into me. Then I spotted an RATP official. And that's when I noticed our suits were the same colour . . .

**M**y ex is a girl from back home, but seeing as she was born in Nancy, you could say she's also a bit French. That's why she never really got it when our people started screeching in the streets around Château d'Eau and Château Rouge. You could see some of them yelling into a telephone box on Rue Strasbourg, shouting themselves hoarse, probably thinking that if they spoke normally then nobody would hear them on the other end of the line. This drove my ex crazy, she used to say she had no time for people like that. It suited me that she got in a huff because I could play on it to go to those Parisian nigger-trash parties on my own, where I'd hunt the wild gazelles turning up for the first time in the capital.

"There's a Congolese party tomorrow night at Garges-lès-Gonesse," I'd say to her, sounding downbeat. "Oh, it won't be anything special, I'll go, but just to show my face, I don't want to get a bad name for myself as a compatriot who thinks he can go it alone now that he's in France. A reputation like that is a serious matter, because the day I die the Congolese won't come to the morgue, they won't club together to repatriate my corpse to the fold. Of course I'd like you to come too, but it won't be your scene, they're expecting several tribes, and not just any old tribes, we're talking the Bembés and the Laris! That lot come straight from the bush, where there's no electricity. I swear they'll be shouting all night until the cops show up, they'll urinate in the main entrance, and that's before we've even got started on them smoking a minimum of two hundred cigarettes an hour, and seeing as you're pregnant, I just thought that . . . "

She cut me short:

"Listen, you can go and see your brothers for yourself! But whatever you do, don't count on me coming or I'll tell them what I think of their boorish behaviour! How can people urinate in front of a building and smoke like that?"

We used to have big arguments about what she took to be fixed truths on the subject of our condition as negroes, when they were just clichés in black and white. It's true I often played up the caricatured version of our customs to my own advantage, so I could go it alone to those crowded parties. But I also set the record straight when I needed to. And bringing down the concrete walls in her mind was no walk in the park. She was convinced, just like Roger the French-Ivorian, that our ancestors were courageous Gauls and that we were all the black grandchildren of Vercingetorix. I'm the one who told her that the muscular, blonde version of Tarzan she'd loved since she was a little girl and who leapt with such ease from creeper to creeper in the company of wild animals was not in fact the king of our jungle; and even that nice, brave, clever Tintin with his quiff had told porky pies about the Congo because, I mean, let's be objective here: do I look like anything like the negroes you see in *The Adventures of Tintin in the Congo*? Those big fat pink lips they stuck on us weren't real Congolese lips, even if certain history books at the time reported we hadn't quite completed the evolutionary process of turning from monkeys into men and that we still scratched our backs with our toes.

But my ex wasn't persuaded by my explanations. She argued with me, saying the opposite was true, she quoted those history books written by Whites between a couple of colonial expeditions and a few battles lost to Shaka Zulu who enjoyed ensnaring them using the old burnt-earth tactic. She would give me a whole patter about beaten earth huts, tree houses and African black magic, about witchcraft that could turn human beings invisible, about swamps that gobbled up trees, about animals roaming free, about the red earth that filthied the faces of children with distended bellies. I replied that we didn't live in that heart of darkness, that there are some Africans who have never seen an elephant or a gorilla, including those who had only ever spotted those kinds of animals in the zoos of Europe or in *King Kong*. So she shouldn't go picturing us keeping wild animals on a leash to take to school with us, and playing with them at break-time before politely accompanying them back to the jungle where their parents would be waiting for us by the banks of the Congo River, so they could thank us for being so kind.

Seeing as she relished my stories about being a kid back in the home country, I also told her about how we survived without toys at Christmas, how we played football with a ball that wasn't round at all, but you still had to shoot straight, and dribble past a group of eleven players, and score goals as if the ball was round. We beat the living daylights out of that ball made of old rags, we wanted to be champions one day because the grown-ups had told us that King Pelé started playing with a flat ball like that and he'd gone on to become the youngest champion at seventeen. He had scored six goals during the World Cup in Sweden in 1956, the grown-ups used to tell us, as if they'd been present in person when the young Brazilian boy-wonder had pulled off that feat. And so we were all Pelés, we dribbled, we made dodgy passes, we tackled imaginary legs, we trapped the ball with our backs and not our chests, we executed volleyed back-heel flicks, our imaginary lines didn't even mark the halfway point, we entered invisible penalty areas where we hoped the opposing team would mow us down so that we'd be granted a penalty which we'd miss because we didn't believe enough in what we were doing. There was no red card because red was the colour of our one and only Party which banned us from showing it to the four winds. So there were only yellow cards, and some players got at least thirty per match because nobody knew what colour card to show a player to get them off the pitch for good. And I explained to my ex how, before those matches, we would go first to the fetish man who made us grigris and promised us that we would be unbeatable. He used to make us sleep in the Mouyondzi district cemetery where the devils don't trifle with football and they come out of their tombs to play in place of the living. And so there was a devil behind each player, and our goals went into the back of the net all by themselves before we'd even touched our flat ball. Sometimes it went in, sometimes it didn't. But when it didn't go in, we wouldn't blame the poor fetish man. He wasn't God. He had done his work and the devils had done theirs. It was our own fault because we never observed what the fetish man had advised us to do on the eve of the match: to wake up in the morning by opening first the right eye, then the left eye; to get out of bed putting the right foot down first; not to touch the genital area for twenty-four hours; not to greet any girls – especially sisters and mothers – until the match was over; not to turn around when someone calls your name, but always wait until they're level with you even if it's your father or your mother; not to let a single drop of rain fall on you – even though our matches only took place during the rainy season. That's how we were, we used to tell ourselves that other youngsters in foreign countries couldn't possibly have more fun than we did, and we were happy in our own world, with our tattered shirts, our worn-out sandals tied to our feet with bits of wire; that's how we were, with holes in our shorts and the whole bazaar of what passes for everyday life among those who had never invented anything, not gunpowder and not the compass, among those who had never known how to tame steam or electricity, among those who had never explored the seas or the sky.

And my ex, who was moved by this, asked:

"Did you make that up, all that stuff about gunpowder, compasses, steam, electricity, the seas and the sky?"

I told her it wasn't me, that these were things we'd learned at school, back in the home country, things Europeans didn't get taught. They came from a man who was angry, a black poet who used to speak courageous words. He had written them on returning to his native country and finding his people hungry, the streets dirty, the rum like dynamite exploding his island, a people who didn't rise up against their condition or the invisible hand that was subjugating them. There could be no messing around with that angry man, since he had also written in black and white: *Because we hate you,*

*you and your reason, we lay claim to dementia praecox, to*
*the blazing madness of inveterate cannibalism . . .*

At which point my ex became very sad. I felt guilty
about leaving her in such low spirits, so then I had to
entertain her with different stories about love, that way
she wouldn't go to sleep with our courageous poet's
ideas about dementia praecox, blazing madness and
inveterate cannibalism.

We were lying in bed, and it was nearly midnight as I
talked to her in my deepest voice. I told her about how
we learnt to sweet-talk girls for the first time. It was
something we were dreading, so we paid a visit to a big
brother in the district who was called Big Poupy because
he was always surrounded by girls and his throat didn't
dry up when he was talking to them. He had chatted
up all sorts of girls: tall ones and short ones, bantam-
weight, featherweight and even super-heavyweight. He
claimed to have an all-areas pass. The girls filed past his
bedroom door, which looked out on to Independence
Avenue. We'd be down below, counting Big Poupy's
victories. He wasn't afraid to touch the girls' hair, to
hold hands with them, and sometimes even to pinch
those buttocks we dreamt about. And these girls
laughed instead of going home to complain to their
parents! At the time we could only stare at girls from a
distance. Our stomachs were in knots, and we wanted
to pee our pants as soon as one of them looked us in

the eye. It was like being felled by an earthquake, and sometimes we'd cry because the emotion of it turned us into salt statues. Another reason for us watching the girls from a distance was that we didn't want any trouble. Our parents had warned us about the wicked and evil scorpion they had in their sexual organ, and about how this scorpion could sting ours.

Which is why all our hopes lay with Big Poupy. We paid him ten Central African CFA francs – he was the one who'd set the rate – for him to teach us what we had to say when we ran into a girl leaving her parents' plot of land to go to the market. According to Big Poupy, you had to raise your head up high, stand straight as a soldier, hold your breath for ten seconds, breathe out gently, and then ask the girl:

"So where are you off to like that?"

And according to Big Poupy the girl's answer would always be:

"I'm going to the market."

We had to raise our heads up high again, stand straight as a soldier, hold our breath for five seconds not ten, and then say in an authoritative voice, while giving them a sidelong glance:

"I'm coming with you! Give me your basket!"

Big Poupy was right. More often than not, the girls agreed to this. But we quickly ran into trouble because we had to talk to them when all the questions Big Poupy had taught us had flown clean out of our heads, things like: How tall are you? How much do you weigh? Have you made love before? What did you have to eat yesterday? Did you sweep your parents' yard before coming out? Are you smart at school? What is the capital of Nepal? What is the surface area of our country? What is a non-aligned country? Was Hitler German or Austrian? What is Victor Hugo's first name?"

We were so surprised to be walking next to a girl that our brains went blank. We tensed up and the way to the market felt very long. And the people who saw us sweating behind the girl assumed we were only carrying her basket because we were her parents' house-boy . . .

When my ex burst out laughing, I quickly added that, over time, we stopped believing in Big Poupy's smooth-talk which cost us a lot for nothing. That's why we ended up going to see a good fetish man in the Trois-Cents district instead, like for those football matches with the balls that weren't at all round. The fetish man would ask us to bring him some hair belonging to the girl and so we'd go and loiter wherever our ladylove was braiding her hair with her friends. Sometimes there'd be half a dozen girls taking it in turns to braid each other's hair. We pretended to help them, we'd do the sweeping up and then, when they weren't looking, we'd steal their locks of hair without knowing whose they were because how can you tell the difference when it comes to a black woman's hair? It's easier in other countries where you've got blondes, brunettes, redheads with or without freckles and I don't know what else. We stole any old lock of hair that was lying on the ground, on the basis that it doesn't matter what colour the cat is provided it catches the mouse. We would run to the fetish man's house with our plunder, he would mix the hairs up with some stuff of his own and chant things we never understood even though we were from the same ethnic group as him. Sometimes it worked, sometimes it didn't.

Since my ex was often incredulous by this stage in my stories and in need of concrete examples, well, I told her that I'd seen with my own eyes how a love fetish had worked well for my childhood friend Placide, whose girlfriend Marceline had cleared off without saying goodbye and taken up with one of our classmates who always got nought out of twenty in Mérimée's dictation, two out of twenty for history and geography, and nineteen and a half out of twenty for physical education thanks to his Beninese fisherman's muscles. Placide, unlike us, had been lucky enough to hear about a proper fetish man who came from a faraway village in the north of the country. This fetish man didn't want a cent upfront, you'll pay after the result he said, I'm not in this for the money. Without saying anything to us, Placide went to see this man who gave him a little seed and told him to plant it in a bowl when he got back home, and to water it every day at around midnight while invoking Marceline's name. Our friend rose at midnight, knelt down in front of his plant, and called out Marceline's name for at least an hour. One week later, when the seed had produced a small shoot, we were all surprised to see Marceline strolling once more in front of the plot of land belonging to Placide's parents. She brought him food now and said she couldn't sleep any more without seeing him, without touching him, without smelling him, without gluing her lips to his just like in the movies we watched at The Rex. None of us in our district got it at all, because what did Placide have that we didn't to turn the head of a beautiful girl like Marceline? The more the plant grew, the more the girl clung to Placide.

A group of us went round to our friend's house so he could at least tell us what district his fetish man from the north lived in because we wanted girls to throw themselves into our arms as well, and to bring us food on our parents' plot of land and to glue their lips to ours just like in the movies. We wanted girls to tell us they couldn't sleep without us any more. But Placide refused to reveal the name of his fetish man, he said it was a secret.

So we all chorused:

"You don't want to give us the name of your fetish man from the north? Well, if that's the way it is, just wait and see what's going to happen to you!"

So that night while he was asleep, we destroyed his

plant, we urinated all over it, flattened it and broke the bowl it was in, just like that.

The next day the sparks really started flying between Placide and Marceline. They bickered like two strangers, hurling insults at each other in front of everybody.

Marceline took up again with her guy who scored low in Mérimée's dictation, as well as history and geography, but high in physical education. We never owned up to destroying Placide's plant. And anyway he never suspected us, because he was convinced it was the muscular dunce himself who was exacting his revenge and who had gone to see the same fetish man to win Marceline back . . .

And lastly, I didn't hide it from my ex that later on, when we were sixteen, we thought you had to write beautiful love letters if you wanted to sweet-talk the girls. The trouble was, you already needed to have read some books with those sorts of letters in them. But what kind of books? Novels? Oh no, they were too long. They never ended, the authors waffled on for hundreds of pages. Plus the characters in the novels we tried reading got on our nerves because they took too much time about it, and they only kissed towards the final pages. We wanted to get there fast, not waste our time describing a blue sky, the birch trees or a migrating bird that doesn't know which branch to land on when it's flying over an entire tropical forest. Luckily, there was *The Perfect Secretary*. That book was our bible. We used to go and read it at the French Cultural Centre in Pointe-Noire, towards the Côte Sauvage. And you had to get up early to be the first to borrow it because we'd noticed that old men came along to copy down things from it as well so they could chat up the local elderly widows . . .

My ex was now sitting up in bed and she wanted to know the name of the author of *The Perfect Secretary*. I told her I'd forgotten, that at the time we didn't bother with the authors' names, we thought they were all dead so what was the point? I explained to her that *The Perfect Secretary* was a collection of letters to help people write their CV or a job application letter, or a letter of condolence in which they were saddened by somebody dying, albeit at the grand old age of a hundred and two. The bit that interested us was at the end of the book: examples of love letters to send to girls. We would copy them out word for word and send them to the girls just like that. But in those template letters from *The Perfect Secretary*, the girls were always white, sometimes they were blonde with blue eyes, or brunette with green eyes or redheaded with freckles. And we sent our letters without even tropicalising them. We told ourselves that love had no colour, and good luck to the person who wanted to give a colour to words and emotions. We wrote about winter, we described the snow, we stuck pine trees into every paragraph. And seeing as our girls liked these words, we ended up thinking that nothing could be more poetic than to call a particularly black girl "My Snowy White" . . .

I even admitted to my ex that my first love has stuck with her pet name of "Snowy White", and that she isn't alone in laying claim to that appellation of uncontrolled origin.

All the girls of my youth were, truth be told, Snowy Whites . . .

My ex had stopped moving. I leaned over and realised she'd been asleep for a while and that I'd been telling this last story to an audience of one.

I switched off the light and soon I was fast asleep too . . .

I had nicknamed her Original Colour on account of her very black skin. Back in the home country, we still believe that negroes born in France are less black than us. But no, as bad luck would have it, before we met I'd never clapped eyes on anyone as black as my ex. There are some people, when you see them, they're black as manganese or tar, so you figure they must have roasted under the tropical sun, but then out of the blue they tell you they were born in France. When it's like that I insist they show me their identity card on the spot. And if I see to my great surprise that they're right, that they really were born in France, even in the middle of a savage winter like Abbé Pierre's winter of 1954, then I fly off the handle. I'm thinking: what world are we living in if people are busy demolishing the little things that keep our prejudices alive, eh? Am I the kind of fool who swallows stories hook, line and sinker? How can you be as black as that and born in France? It's unthinkable. It's outrageous. It shouldn't be allowed. It flies in the face of nature. What is the point of braving the winter and the snow if it's not to wash the skin of the Blacks and make it a bit whiter?

So anyway, my ex – who I'm going to call Original Colour from now on – really was born that dark . . .

* * *

I saw Original Colour for the first time opposite Jip's, three and a half years ago. It never crossed my mind that a few months later we'd be living together, and that she would become the mother of my daughter. At the time she was working at Soul Fashion, a ladies' underwear shop with fluorescent thongs on display right out into the street – something else that would have shocked our Arab on the corner.

From the counter in Jip's, you could see what was happening at Soul Fashion – sometimes we even caught a glimpse of girls trying on thongs, we'd give a running commentary and smirk when they walked in front of the bar . . .

That first day when I met my ex, I was smartly dressed, with Westons on my feet and a made-to-measure Valentino Uomo suit. The girl was pacing up and down in front of Soul Fashion, a cigarette dangling from her lips. Most of my pals were there, some standing out on the terrace like me, others leaning on the counter, one eye on their glass and the other on the street. I can picture their faces as if it were yesterday. There was Roger the French-Ivorian, who likes to make out he's read all the books in the world. There was Yves "the just-Ivorian", who likes to shout it from the rooftops that he came to France to make French women pay back the colonial debt and that he will succeed by all means necessary. There was Vladimir the Cameroonian who smokes the longest cigars in France and Navarre. There was Paul from the big Congo, who likes to splash on aftershaves before they're available on the open market – we also call him the 'Holy Bust' because he's always going on about how buttocks aren't the only thing in life, there are breasts too. . . . I can see Pierrot the White from the small Congo, the self-proclaimed "Word specialist" who reckons the Bible is lying to us, that in the beginning there wasn't just the Word, but also the verb and the subject and the direct object, and it was Man who added the indirect object for he'd had enough of worshipping a divinity who could never be seen. And I can see Olivier from the small Congo, who's got slanting eyes but who can still see everything coming from a way off, especially the girls. As for our other compatriot, Patrick "the Scandinavian", he married a Finnish girl and they've got a kid I haven't met yet.

And finally I'm seeing that nutter Bosco again, "the wandering Chadian", who writes everybody off as ignoramuses because he's convinced that he's got the highest intelligence quota in Africa, and that he alone can master the subtleties of the imperfect subjunctive. How can a man who calls himself civilised go and urinate against the walls of Jip's when there are toilets in this bar and even

passers-by come to piss here without buying a drink? He
calls himself a lyrical poet, he reads us dusty verses he claims
to have written as a student at a lycée in Ndjamena where
he got bored in the midst of all those dunces. According to
him, it's thanks to his flair for verse-writing that he won a
scholarship from the French Embassy in Chad, the French
having judged unanimously that his place was no longer in
Africa but in France and that our poet was unequivocally
the long-awaited "black Paul Valéry". So we call him "The
Embassy Poet", and he talks with this Parisian accent that
makes Pierrot the White declare our Chadian in search of
lost time to be a paper negro who is still in the process of
being colonised, which explains why he's got black skin
and a white mask . . .

They were all there. They were making remarks about
Original Colour under the complicit watch of Jeannot
the owner and Willy the barman, who was pumping
out furious music from I don't know which squalid
quarter of Abidjan, Dakar, Douala or Brazzaville.
     They saw me heading over to Soul Fashion and
having a chat with Original Colour. I was trying to read
the name on her badge, she had a surname from back
home and Willy enjoyed seizing every opportunity to
make fun of it:
     "I know that girl, she got hired not long ago. Her
surname is so complicated you need an extra bone in
the back of your throat to pronounce it . . . "

Apart from her tar-baby skin, which my friends gave me a hard time about – because back home we're not so keen on skin like that – I noticed she had an amazing asset: her backside moved in an anti-clockwise direction. Now, it's not any old backside that has a talent like that. To this day, when I'm out strolling in the street, I watch the girls' backsides closely in the hope of seeing if God made another of the same build and suppleness. I've come to the conclusion that works of art are one-offs which can't be imitated, especially if the artist in question is God himself. Later on, when we were out walking together, I would always make sure I was behind Original Colour, like her shadow, I'd pretend to be taking my time, to drop my keys, to pick them up and all that without taking my eyes off the show-stopper in front of me because I didn't want to miss out on a single movement of her booty-crammed bodywork. Original Colour would turn around, smile at me, and speed up the movements of her B-side even more while my heart leapt like a baby kangaroo over-excited by a passing jeep. I thought about how lucky she was to have a backside with automatic gears because, and you may not have noticed this, but not everybody got provided for in that department. Mother Nature gave some women special treatment, and was a right bitch to others . . .

It's definitely Original Colour who increased my obsession with backsides. From our first encounter, they were all I could think about. So, instead of walking with my head up like everybody else, I developed a thing for feasting my eyes on the lower backs of the girls walking by, followed by a full and in-depth analysis. I am now convinced that, as with neckties, you can understand human psychology from the way people shift their rear-ends. So it's no big surprise that at Jip's most of my pals call me "Buttologist". It was Pierrot the White who came up with this neologism – although I don't believe in neologisms given there's nothing new under the sun. The science of the backside has been around since the beginning of the world when Adam and Eve turned their backs on the Lord. Each time Pierrot the White gets a new girlfriend, he brings her double-quick to Jip's, buys her a drink, and whispers in my ear to have a good ogle of her rear extension and fatty-muscle tissues so that we can talk about it later on, because he doesn't want to bark up the wrong tree and land himself a pain in the neck and all because of a non-starter of a backside. Then, once the girl heads off, Pierrot the White runs over and asks me what I thought. He adds that it excites him when I'm talking about it. And so I remind him about all the different types of B-sides. I tell him there are some backsides that disappoint when you see them move, you ask yourself: is this really a backside I'm seeing? You feel sorry for it because you can't tell which direction it's going in, because it hasn't got a face, because it swings to the left but never to the right, as if that way danger lay, because it returns abruptly to its starting point, because it flattens out, because it comes to a stop without a hint of elegance. It's like that when the girl is uptight, when she can never reach a decision without talking about it first to her girlfriends, who will always lead her astray. I point out there's another type of backside, and its problem is moving up and down too quickly like an angry gecko, so the poor woman has to pull up her trousers or her skirt at every juncture. If you get chatting to a girl who has to lug that kind of fatty-muscle tissue around behind her, you'll notice that she becomes aggressive for no reason, she arranges non-dates at the fountain by Saint-Michel or the Church of Saint-Bernard, she doesn't show up and then she dumps you by sending a special delivery signed-for letter. I also point out to Pierrot the White that some backsides are even worse, they are clenched, and instead of moving they judder, they tremble, they're epileptic, and then they stall. Backsides like that have manual gears and, in general, they're flat as a spanking new motorway. You can find these types of backsides among certain intellectual women who drive you to distraction only to tell you at the end of the day that they need some time to think it over, to conduct their own internal review and to finish reading up on transcendental theories as postulated in Kant's *Critique of Pure Reason* . . .

As for me, I was one happy man, in Original Colour I had found the butt of my dreams, I was king of the hill and cock of the walk . . .

* * *

Words couldn't do justice to Original Colour's B-side, but she had a face of stone to discourage someone approaching her for the first time. Not that I had anything to lose, her stony face was hardly Mount Everest, and her scornful expression was just her natural way of protecting herself, like porcupines brandishing their spines to scare off predators. I took my courage in my hands, walked towards her, saw her smile – I'm guessing it was my get-up because she looked me up and down – and that's how we started chatting in front of Soul Fashion.

I quickly sensed that I shouldn't ask her too much about Africa, she wasn't familiar with it. Or with the Congo either. She dreamed of going there one day, whereas I just had to remember my eventful arrival in France fifteen years earlier and my life before that as a packer in the port of Pointe-Noire to know that I never wanted to go back. Although I kept it to myself, I was shocked to discover that she was born here given how dark she was. I was this close to asking to see her identity card, but I didn't want to offend her. She saw I couldn't take my eyes off her backside. As a buttologist I was trying to figure out her behaviour, but for once I was out of luck because surgeons don't operate on themselves. Clairvoyants can't read their own futures. Better still, to use a ready-made phrase, cobblers are always the worst shod. So I settled for studying that black well-oiled skin, it was glowing: "My God," I wondered, "how has she managed to end up as dark as that, when we're not short on winters in this country . . . ?"

That day I already wanted to stake out my territory, get the words flowing between us. I wasn't going to ask her the kind of questions Big Poupy used to teach us when we were very young and wanted to chat up girls. Over all, I didn't handle it too badly. My pals at Jip's gave me a round of applause when I returned with Original Colour's telephone number. But they were just winding me up, especially Yves the just-Ivorian who pointed out that I'd never make France pay back its colonial debt with a girl like that . . .

\* \* \*

We found ourselves talking more and more, almost every other day – I'd let at least a day go by, sometimes two, I didn't want her to feel pressurised in any way. The girl I was getting to know was kind and sweet and attentive. I invited her out to different bars and cafés around Les Halles because my pals were getting on my nerves now, applauding me as if I'd won a world record in I don't know what sport.

We visited everywhere in the 1st arrondissement: Le Père Tranquille, Le Baiser Salé, La Chapelle des Lombards, Oz Café and I can't remember where else.

Sometimes she really made me laugh. Back then, just as later on when the Arab on the corner used to tell us his jokes about the Israelis feeling blue or "mo' sad" because of the gloomy weather, or the North Africans using the "Kabyle" telephone to call home, I was mainly laughing at the way she laughed, she sounded like a clapped-out car that couldn't manage a hill-start any more, she really went for it and the tears would pour down her face. Sometimes she would come and have a drink with me up at the counter in Jip's. The guys stared at her backside from a safe distance and reckoned that, for a buttologist, I'd made a boob, that I didn't know what I was letting myself in for.

"Why are they laughing like that?" she would ask me, tilting her head in the direction of Roger the French-Ivorian, Willy the barman and Yves the just-Ivorian.

"They're being kids," would be my answer.

Despite their jibes, I approached the girl's penalty area, and I kept going, eyes closed, convinced I was in the right, and that the others were blind men without white sticks. Did Bosco the Chadian Poet and Pierrot the White from the small Congo really have anything to teach me on the subject? I didn't appreciate it when Yves the just-Ivorian gave me a hard time in front of everybody:

"Wake up, Buttologist! We're in France here and you've got real goals to score because an away goal always counts as two points, my friend. But you've chosen the easy path, going for a compatriot. Is this how you intend to make the people of this country compensate us for everything they inflicted on us during colonisation, eh? They stripped us of our primary resources, so we've got to steal their treasures, and by that I mean their women! So ditch that fat-arsed sun-roasted woman of yours and bag a pretty blonde with blue or green eyes, you can't move for them in the streets of Paris and beyond. And another thing, those White girls won't give you a hard time compared to our sisters who are first-class pains in the neck. It's her butt that's making you lose your head like this, isn't it? Well then pay a visit to where I come from, in the Ivory Coast, and you will see what a real woman's backside looks like, how it moves, how it trembles, how it rotates like the blades of a helicopter. The girl I see smoking in front of Soul Fashion is just a tiny mirage, you'll be disappointed the day she takes off those trousers of hers because her butt will collapse all the way down to her calves . . .

I didn't take kindly either to the remarks of Vladimir the Cameroonian who smokes the longest cigars in France and Navarre. He made it clear that in order to satisfy Original Colour my thing down there would have to be as long as two of his cigars stuck together.

"Buttologist, have you seen how long my cigar is, eh? Does it remind you of anything?"

I didn't react.

"Now, I'm going to take another cigar out of my pocket and I'm going to stick them end to end like this. Look . . . !"

And then Vladimir finished off with:

"You'll need a tool as big as that, you see, or the girl will laugh in your face. And you can count your lucky stars I haven't managed to get hold of the longest cigar in the world yet, made by the Cuban José Castelar and measuring eleven metres and four centimetres! You're just a Sapper, a dandy, a lover of Westons and suits from the Rue du Faubourg-Saint-Honoré. Back in the Cameroon, we say that length isn't so much of a Congolese attribute. My advice to you is get fit!"

But I decided to go with the advice of Paul from the big Congo, who told me I should do the business and then beat it at the first opportunity . . .

Later on, I would find out from Original Colour that her parents lived in Nancy where they had a lawyers' practice, that only French was spoken at home and that she didn't understand a single one of the hundreds of languages in our country. Her father was opposed to the regime in power, and consequently he was banned from entering the Congo, but he hoped that one day it would be his turn to become President of our Republic, and then he would snatch our oil from the hands of the French and give it to the Americans instead. He would crush all the northerners and throw them into the Congo River because he believes his tribe has been experiencing nothing short of genocide for decades now and that this has been met with indifference from the international community. According to the lawyer from Nancy, the only hope for the Congo is for half the country to break away, or else the extermination plain and simple of those from the North who have confiscated the reins of power since Independence and who steal the gas from the South in order to sell it off at a knock-down price to the French. According to Original Colour, her father still had a big grey beard like most African rebels who copied the look of the Angolan resistance fighter of the day, Jonas Savimbi, a charismatic man who, right up until his death, prevented his rival, President Eduardo Dos Santos, from sleeping soundly at night.

Original Colour harboured a grudge against her father. And that spark of hatred would flare up as soon as I tried to find out a bit more about him. She sounded very vexed on the subject. She used to say: "That pro-slaver", "that creature", "that tribalist", "that person I don't know" and even "that man who calls himself my father". According to her, this lawyer was just a Southern extremist, a man who cultivated intolerance even in his own home, a political fanatic whose wife soaked up his words without raising her voice. He would receive at home the bosses of our former regime, which was now shot to pieces following two civil wars. The lawyer and his frustrated guests would ponder a new political party in order to win back power, by force if needs be. He was waiting on the green light from America because, he maintained, these days you can't have political change in any French-speaking country in Africa without the help of the Yankees given that the French kept everything under lock and key in their former colonies . . .

* * *

I'd had to push for Original Colour to explain how she'd ended up on her own in Paris instead of living in Nancy. She had fallen out with her father – and so, on the rebound, with her mother too – on account of a marriage deal that her parents had struck with Doyen Methuselah, our former Finance Minister back in the home country, the one who had emptied the state coffers when he realised that the regime in which he was a senior minister wouldn't survive the second civil war, because the new strong man in the country had the support of France as well as more tanks, missiles, helicopters and rockets than the regular army. And so Doyen Methuselah had fled in great haste across the Congo River together with the ex-president, before catching a plane to Belgium, then France where he was accorded the status of a political exile. The minister liked to proclaim it from the Paris rooftops that he could feed every member of the Congolese opposition living in France, including those in Corsica and Monaco, for a hundred and fifty years. The Congolese in France would visit him at his private mansion in the 8th arrondissement and leave clutching big fat envelopes stuffed with notes. His fortune was estimated to equal the entire debt of our country. So all he had to do was give back to the people what he had stolen and then our nation could stop snivelling at the summits of rich countries about getting our debt cancelled. But Doyen Methuselah led the high life in France. He threw private parties in grand palaces where, in the middle of the night, he would have his wicked way with young Congolese girls barely out of puberty. Doyen Methuselah was very close to Original Colour's father, who had defended him in a trial about embezzling public monies that had made a lot of noise in France a while back, and he had set his heart on the daughter of his former lawyer and his friend. He wanted to marry her despite the thirty-eight years that separated them. This would have tied things up nicely for the lawyer from Nancy who was hoping to benefit from the financial support of Doyen Methuselah so as to strengthen his political party while waiting for the green light from the Yankees.

Original Colour wanted to turn the page. So I didn't ask her any more questions on the subject. She talked to me instead about one of her childhood friends, Rachel Kouamé, who had left Nancy for Paris ahead of her. They had been inseparable from elementary school all the way through to lycée. The day before Original Colour, in accordance with her father's wishes, was supposed to marry Doyen Methuselah she packed her bags for Paris and went to knock on the door of her childhood friend . . .

* * *

Looking back on it, I think it must have been Rachel Kouamé who had spoilt her. The Ivorian girl was a bit older than Original Colour and rented a studio on Rue Dejean, in the heart of Château Rouge market where she sold saltfish, having abandoned her chaotic studies in accountancy. The two girls were now working together.

They bought their saltfish from a Chinese wholesaler in Rue de Panama and sold it piecemeal, on the ground, at the fringes of the market between police raids. But their business demanded patience without turning in much of a profit. Plus their stall had to be very portable, with the result that it was often just a box so they could pack it away again and take to their heels at the first sound of a police car.

Original Colour observed the Château Rouge community and how it lived. After a few months, she came to the conclusion that we Africans spent astronomical sums on whitening our skin. That we would rather die of hunger than put up with dark skin.

One evening, when their business had been struggling for some time, she suggested to Rachel that they try their hand at selling de-negrifying products:

"We can sell this stuff, I know where to buy Ambi rouge and Diprosone at heavily discounted prices. This trade is like being an undertaker: undertakers are never out of work because people are condemned to die. Well, it's the same with us Blacks: we'll never give up trying to lighten our skin as long as we're convinced that the curse hanging over us is simply a matter of colour . . . "

* * *

Unlike Original Colour, Rachel wasn't cut out to be a businesswoman. She bullied her customers and chased after the latest Paris fashions, which she would flaunt in the nightclubs of Abidjan during the Christmas holidays. A chronic big-spender, she squandered their joint savings. Without warning her friend, Rachel would go off to the Champs-Elysées or Rue du Faubourg-Saint-Honoré on shopping sprees, returning with bulging bags of clothes and luxury shoes. She couldn't wear it all, so she sold on clothes and shoes from past seasons to her friends in Abidjan. She knew all about a taste for luxury. She bought her jewellery at Cartier on Place Vendôme, and wanted to wear the same perfume as Cathérine Deneuve, Juliette Binoche and Vanessa Paradis. She was finding it harder and harder to justify her spending when Original Colour demanded they do their accounts and look into expanding their small business to reach other Blacks from further afield than Château Rouge and Château d'Eau. Their arguments became more frequent, and at one point the two friends and business associates didn't speak for a week. Each cooked for herself in a corner of the room, without bothering about the other. Original Colour swallowed her pride and tried to strike up a conversation, but she could barely get a word out of Rachel. In the end, Original Colour was made to feel that she was to blame for her business partner's mismanagement. They lost the goodwill of their suppliers who refused to deliver on credit. It was cash only from now on. But the coffers were empty . . .

Relations were already tense between the two girls, and they deteriorated further when Rachel imposed a man on the household. Like her he was from the Ivory Coast, and he had the muscles of a fisherman of the open sea. But it turned out he was a shrewd gigolo who became lethally violent when drunk, smashing the crockery, and threatening to set the entire building on fire. This lout moved into Rachel's place where he considered himself master of the premises. When he returned from his trips out and about, his food had to be ready with Rachel at home to serve it to him and massage his feet. Then he would collapse on the sofa-bed in front of the television, legs splayed. He would watch the football on Canal Plus, or else the pornographic film broadcast by the same channel on the first Saturday of every month. Unable to put up with this any more, Original Colour gave him a piece of her mind one evening when Rachel was there.

The Ivorian was quick to put her down:

"Since when a woman does have the right to speak, you'd think a man like that, eh? Is a woman same on a man? Who you are taking you for, isn't it? Are you even coming up to my ankles? Is your small French you talk bad going to push me out? Have seen your big fat bumper moving in the crowd like a black snake in a Camara Laye story cutted in half? If you don't agree, get out our house! I spit on your race! You are not here at home, you bloody Congolese girl from Bacongo . . . !"

Because Rachel did nothing to put this predatory scum in his place, Original Colour came to the conclusion that she was a crowd in their two-room apartment.

After a heated argument with her friend who defended her man tooth and nail, Original Colour packed up her belongings during the week, and rented a room in a cheap hotel on Rue de Suez, which was mainly occupied by Nigerian female stallholders from the Marché Dejean. She was quickly introduced into the network of women who imported de-negrifying products from back home. And they wasted little time in adopting the young Congolese woman, because she helped them write the letters and fill out the forms in French that are a necessary part of everyday life. Original Colour became, if you like, their public writer . . .

* * *

Living alongside these Nigerian women was no easy ride. Petty squabbles about twice nothing set the girls against one another. Boyfriend trouble or something to do with witchcraft. As soon as one of the Nigerian ladies brought a man onto the premises, the others were all competing to sleep with him.

And then there were the nocturnal catfights. The police would turn up, sirens blaring fit to burst the eardrums of the crowd gathered in front of the building. The Nigerian ladies would threaten each other with pestles, forks and sometimes even with cans of caustic soda. Some ended up with faces streaked with deep scars. Was there still room for Original Colour, caught in the middle of all these frenzied females? The young French-Congolese woman needed to win her independence back. Around this time, on the stairs of their hotel, she met a man who said that he owned a ladies' underwear shop in Les Halles. The man was a regular client of the Nigerian ladies. I never found out exactly what kind of relationship he had with Original Colour. She was very evasive on the subject. But what I do know is that from one day to the next the man hired her to work at Soul Fashion.

She started looking for somewhere to live and found a studio in the 18th arrondissement, which meant burning her bridges with her Nigerian friends who accused her of stealing their man who "paid handsomely" and didn't haggle . . .

As soon as Original Colour appeared in front of Soul Fashion, I used to break off my conversation with my pals, leave my glass of Pelfort and rush over to her. I made sure I wore my most elegant suits, for the sole purpose of charming her, and she liked it because she knew about the Sapper scene and Château Rouge. She used to say I was the real deal, a Congolese man from head to toe. And as she said it, she would point to my tie and my Westons. Not only that but why hide it, she liked to hear me talking about my plans. And she wondered what on earth I was doing in that bar instead of continuing with my studies, since I'd made it into the final year at school. And my reply would be that I didn't want to waste my time with a bunch of kids in a lecture theatre. I'm a trend-setter, I live my life to the full . . .

\* \* \*

When three days went by without my showing up at Jip's, Original Colour would go into the bar and ask Paul from the big Congo who, in her eyes, was the person in our group most likely to take her seriously, whether he

had any news about me. The truth was, I was waiting
for her to call, which she used to do late at night. And
we would talk for ages. It seems I made her laugh a
lot, and she melted at my accent. It was that very deep
accent from back home, the same as her father's – but
she never made the connection, even though later on I
would hear it in his voice on the phone. I rolled my R's
on purpose just to please her. I could switch effortlessly
from a deep voice to a high-pitched voice because it's
not rocket science for a negro to play at being a negro.
Just go with the flow: what's bred in the bone comes
out in the flesh.

Out of all the French restaurants we ate at together,
her favourite was Le Pied de Cochon because she loved
pork. I thought it was a shame the restaurant didn't
sell cassava because to serve pork without cassava is
committing a heinous crime in my ethnic group. We
used to eat there at least three times a week. The waiters
knew us and would often give us a table on the first
floor, by the window.

After the meal, our route was all mapped out: we'd
chat along the banks of the Seine, and I'd tell her to
open her eyes wide and admire the place where a poet
had become very famous because he reminded these
blind Parisians that under the Pont Mirabeau flowed
the Seine. Otherwise they'd never have known, with
their crazy rat-race lives.

On the way back, we'd have a last drink at the Sarah

Bernhardt. We'd stroll a bit before catching the métro at Étienne Marcel. I'd get out at Château d'Eau, while she carried on to Marcadet Poissonniers where she changed for Marx Dormoy.

* * *

One day, when she wanted to find out at all costs where I lived, given that I'd remained silent on the subject and was always the one who went round to hers, I admitted that I hadn't invited her back to mine because I'd been sharing a tiny studio in Château d'Eau with my fellow countrymen ever since I'd arrived in France. There were five of us in there living like rats, but not from the same family. Each of us had cornered off an area to store our things. We'd take it in turns to cook, or else head to the Congolese restaurants in the banlieues to eat food from our country and down the Pelforts until we'd forgotten the way home. I told her about how one time we'd walked all the way from Sarcelles back to Paris because we'd missed the last RER and the mini-cab firms we called sent us packing, saying their drivers often got bludgeoned by riff-raff in the area or else had teargas grenades thrown in their faces and their takings stolen. By the time we got to Château d'Eau we looked like corpses from the war of 1914–18, we couldn't feel our feet any more and we slept for a day and a half.

"I've been living in a ground floor studio for the past fifteen years. I found it and the others came to join me because it was starting to get expensive living there on my own," I explained to her.

She declared that living for fifteen years in a small room like that was intolerable. She wanted to know if any of my roommates were girls. I could see where she was heading. Another case of the green-eyed monster. I burst out laughing because I suddenly remembered our bumpy ride on that front. We'd had to put up a girl fresh from the home country who was in a fix, the people who'd encouraged her to come over were hot-air merchants who never showed up when she landed at Roissy airport. Her name was Louzolo and she wasn't bad-looking, except for the fact that she had one buttock bigger than the other, which made it look like she was only walking on one side. We knew her from back home and we decided it would be inhuman to leave a compatriot to die in the middle of winter even if she did have one buttock bigger than the other. I don't know what would have happened to her if we hadn't taken her in. She'd been sensible enough to bring with her the telephone numbers of a few compatriots in Paris, and I was on the list. The other people on the list had moved on or else they didn't pick up. So I was her last hope.

She called me at six o'clock in the morning, and I went to fetch her from the airport. We didn't hear a squeak from those hot-air merchants for ten days, still less from the other guys whose telephone numbers she'd scribbled down in an address book that was crumpled from her thumbing the pages so many times. The guys who were meant to put her up had boasted about a large apartment overlooking the Champ de Mars and how when they were brushing their teeth or shaving they had a view of the Eiffel Tower. Since Louzolo was disappointed to see that I lived in a small studio despite leaving our home country more than a decade ago, I apologised in the first instance for living in a neighbourhood that didn't have the Champ de Mars, and then I told her my motto: my glass may be small, but I can drink out of it. And so she stayed with us, but she did miss that view of the Eiffel Tower . . .

Having Louzolo in the studio made us change our habits. We didn't sleep well any more because when she took her shower or slept on her front, half-naked, with her legs slightly apart, all we could think about was our thing down there. There were even those among us who went as far as sniffing her knickers, especially Lokassa aka "Centre Forward" who boasted about having a thing down there that was bigger than all the rest of ours put together. We got bored of him in the end because I couldn't see how he did the business if he spent the whole time revealing his battle secrets, and making out he could draw faster than Lucky Luke and his shadow. Each time he laid it on thick about his performance and his exceptionally long thing down there, it reminded me of that clever man who once said a tiger does not proclaim his tigritude, he pounces on his prey and devours it. Centre Forward didn't know about this because IQ wasn't his speciality. You could see him laying his traps from a mile off. He would come home earlier than the rest of us just to be alone with Louzolo and wait for her to cave in.

"I will succeed," he warned us, "because each time I look at that girl my thing down there rises up all by itself without my brain blowing the whistle! I know what I'm like, and it's a sign that never lets me down. When I see a girl and I get a hard-on, it means she'll end up in my arms. And another thing, between you and me, boys, she's been here ten days already, so she'll reach the point where she's gagging for it. She's not going to let her low countries down there freeze in the middle of winter. Central heating is all well and good, but natural warmth is better!"

Centre Forward waited for the girl to fall into his arms, but the moment never came. He became aggressive, and threatened not to contribute to the water and electricity bills any more. He used to sulk in the evenings and reckoned I was the one who was thwarting his plans, that I was pulling underhand tricks outside our studio, in the cat-houses on Rue des Petites Écuries.

But it was a guy from outside, a Central African with red eyes who finally won the game. He met Louzolo at the Marché Dejean and she bid us farewell one evening, to the great disappointment of Centre Forward who had at least succeeded in stealing a pair of the girl's knickers . . .

I also told Original Colour the names of my roommates at the time. Lokassa aka Centre Forward worked on building sites. He didn't have any papers and was using the identity card of Sylvio, a French Caribbean guy who I ran into sometimes at Jip's. The trouble was that Centre Forward couldn't receive his salary directly. It was paid into Sylvio's bank account, and so the two men had to meet up at the end of every month outside Métro Château d'Eau. Sylvio would draw the money out from his bank and hand it over to Centre Forward, after taking ten per cent commission for the use of his identity card.

Serge was a section supervisor in a branch of Leclerc in the banlieue. Thanks to him we ate decent meat and didn't have to buy light bulbs or toilet paper for our studio. He'd struck a deal with the security guys at his supermarket and could take whatever goods he liked.

Euloge was a security guard at the Bercy 2 Shopping Centre. In his spare time he played the guitar in an orchestra with folks from the big Congo. We didn't like it when he smoked his joints in the toilet. The smell hung around for weeks.

Moungali was a packer in a shoe shop. We turned down the shoes he tried to give us because they weren't Westons. Sometimes, he would fly off the handle about this. To keep the peace, we'd accept his presents and send them back to the home country.

Everybody thought I had a slacker's desk job because I worked at a printing works in Issy-les-Moulineaux. What they didn't realise was that I spent my time loading boxes of magazines and books into vans . . .

Despite all this, Original Colour wanted to come and see the conditions we were living in. My heart skipped a beat. For me it was just a dormitory, there was no question of her visiting me there. She'd have a fainting fit because she'd see that even though I was always clean and well-dressed with the most expensive clothes in France, I slept in a pigsty. There weren't any tables or chairs, there were just mattresses on the floor which we piled up on top of each other every morning so we could move around a bit.

For weeks on end I did everything to stop her from setting foot there. So I was the one who used to go over to hers, to visit this studio where I now live all by myself, ever since she cleared off with our daughter because of the Hybrid who plays African drums in a group nobody's ever heard of in France, including in Corsica and Monaco . . .

* * *

When I walked into the main entrance of Original Colour's building, I was puzzled to hear breathing coming from behind the apartment door next to hers.

"There's someone spying on us from behind that door!" I said in alarm.

"Oh, forget about it, it's just the neighbour again. You met him the other day. I think he's got issues, he's always like that. He doesn't like Blacks."

"But he's as black as we are!"

"There are plenty of Blacks like him who don't know they're black. That's their choice . . ."

Every time there was the slightest noise it set me on edge, and Original Colour started to get fed up:

"I told you, it's my neighbour, so give it a rest . . . Listen, why don't you come and live with me, then we can really get up the bastard's nose. There'll be two negroes from the Congo in the building, and that's not counting the ones who live nearby!"

I thought she was joking. The next day I didn't go to work, I brought my suitcases of clothes and Westons over to her studio. The man we would later nickname Mr Hippocratic kept a close eye on me secretly moving in, and he started breathing more and more heavily behind his door because he could sniff out the nigger-trash laying siege to the building.

From that day on, I only had to poke my face outside to land on him. I would always say hello but he eyed me contemptuously, refusing to answer. When he did open his mouth, it was to tell me to make less noise at night because he could hear us when we were in bed.

"And anyway, what are you doing here, eh? It's a studio, it's not meant for two people!"

Every time I entered the building, my heart would be pounding, I had to go on tiptoes. But I might as well not have bothered because Mr Hippocratic seemed to be expecting me. He would cough to signal that he nothing escaped him. After that I decided not to give a monkey's, and not to credit him with more power than he had. So I walked proud and tall, deliberately making the hall ring out with the sound of my Westons. I whistled a tune from back home and opened the door as loudly as possible.

And he would bellow at the top of his voice:

"Go back to that Congolese bush where you come from!"

Seven months on from meeting each other, Original Colour invited me out for a meal at L'Equateur, a Cameroonian restaurant in the 11th arrondissement where one of her friends was a waitress. It was the first time she'd offered to pay. Her friend welcomed us and pointed to the table opposite the bar. That way she could keep an eye on us. I chose the first dish that caught my eye, ndolé with beef. I'd never eaten it before, but it sounded like saka-saka, a cassava leaf dish from back home. Original Colour just ordered chicken wings and salad. The restaurant had photos displayed of the celebrities who had dined there. I spotted Manu Dibango's smile and Yannick Noah's dreadlocks.

We ate in a silence I began to find heavy and I was trying to figure out what was going on in Original Colour's mind, given she didn't really go to African restaurants much. Something was up, I could tell. Seeing as she couldn't look me in the eye, I guessed straight away:

"You're pregnant . . ."

I glanced in the direction of her friend at the bar. She smiled at me.

"Did she know about this?"

Original Colour didn't answer.

"If I've got this right, we'll need to move apartments?" I ventured.

"You must be joking, rents are expensive in Paris! We'll just have to squeeze all three of us in."

"We could always move out to the banlieue."

"DON'T TALK TO ME ABOUT THE BAN-LIEUE!!! It's a pile of shit out there!"

To this day, I still haven't figured out why the word banlieue got such a reaction out of her. The people on the next table turned around when she started shouting. I chalked it up to the stress of being pregnant. One man even piped up:

"I'm from the banlieue, now d'you think I could eat my meal in peace?"

I wasn't well paid at the printing works, so I needed to supplement my income. At the weekends I would go and buy clothes in Italy, which I quickly sold on to my compatriots in Château Rouge. I brought back suits and ties. Given that everybody knew about my taste for Sappe, there was no shortage of customers. They would follow me to the foot of our building, or else wait for me in front of the Arab on the corner's. As a special favour, my former roommates from Château Rouge got to drink beer with me inside our studio. Mr Hippocratic saw red and took to impersonating the police in front of the main entrance. He demanded to see the identity cards of my customers.

I would react violently:

"You're not the police!"

"As for you, bringing all the illegal immigrants in France and the neighbouring countries into this building! You're going to hear me out!"

*  *  *

I'd like to make it clear that I'm the one who bought the baby clothes, because I wanted Original Colour to know I was the responsible type, that's how it works back home, the man pays for everything, full stop. If I hadn't paid for the baby clothes, my status would be rock bottom today. I wouldn't be able to look myself in the mirror. I also noticed that baby clothes weren't within everyone's means. Those tiny bootees cost an arm and a leg, and the pram was the price of rent back in the home country. You can reproach me for whatever you like, but I'm proud that I protected my honour as a father.

When our little girl was born, I was the happiest father on earth. And I wanted the whole world to know about it. I paid for an announcement in the columns of *Libération* as well as *Le Parisien*, even though babies come into the world anonymously in our circles, as if the parents were ashamed of their progeny. People saw me out and about in the neighbourhood with my pram and a pack of Pampers. I'd be coming back from the Arab on the corner's, I let him talk to my daughter because he said at that age children could understand all the languages in the world. So he spoke to her in Arabic without translating for me . . .

* * *

I didn't wait three months before turning up with my kid at Jip's to show her off to my pals, so they could see with their own eyes that I'd become a dad. They were the ones who had insisted on it, they gave me a hard time about hiding my daughter like those members of my tribe who only show their child several months later so as to avoid evil people putting a curse on them. I told them all they needed to do was read the newspapers in this country, that there was an announcement in *Libération* and *Le Parisien*.

Bosco the Embassy Poet was the first to see my little girl. He was standing at the entrance with a glass of red wine in one hand and a copy of Rimbaud in the other. There was a moment's silence, then he stepped away from the door and stared at us tensely. I nodded to indicate he could hold my child, that I wouldn't mind.

"Have you taken leave of your senses?"

I couldn't understand why he'd reacted like this. It turns out that in Chad, in his ethnic group, the men won't touch a baby until it's twelve months old.

"Don't be offended, my friend. I shall write for your

daughter a poem in the style of Victor Hugo's *Infantile Influence*. And you will see, I promise, that there will be some highly rewarding rhymes from start to finish! The trouble with today's poets is that they have abandoned rhyme. So anyone can call himself a poet, and there is no way of separating the wheat from the chaff. I find it absolutely staggering when I read what these so-called poets write these days. Where has the elegance of Valéry gone? What has happened to the genius of Hugo? What have they done with the impertinence of Baudelaire? Could you tell me, please? I am the only one to stand up against this dereliction of poetic duty. But be there only one poet left, I shall be that poet. Let us place the order for your baby straightaway, here is my pen and a piece of paper to write it down. Would you prefer alexandrines or six-line stanzas? Or rather do not worry yourself, I shall write two versions, one with alexandrines, and another with six-line stanzas. Just allow time for my inspiration to take hold."

To this day, I still haven't received any poem.

As for Vladimir the Cameroonian with the longest cigars in France and Navarre, he joked that two of his cigars end-to-end were longer than my daughter was tall. Not only that but he wanted to know why we had called her Henriette. I told him it was after my grandmother, Henriette Nsoko, a woman who played a very important role in my childhood, and someone I miss a great deal.

My mother and I used to go to see her in the village of
Louboulou in the south of the Congo, she died when I
was barely six years old. The picture I still have of her is
of an old woman sitting in front of the door to her hut,
her eyes raised to the sky as if she were putting herself in
God's hands for the rest of her days. The goats were her
only confidantes, old age had worn away at her memory
and she could no longer remember who I was. When I
opened her kitchen door, she shrieked that she was being
robbed, the villagers would rush over to explain that I was
her grandson, the son of her daughter Pauline Kengué,
not a goat-rustler. But my grandmother, doubtful and
suspicious, would fret:

"Who is Pauline Kengué?"

This wasn't how Vladimir saw it:

"I understand that Henriette was your grandmother's
name, but there's no need to go overboard! With all the
names that are available in the Whites' calendar, how
dare you condemn the poor little girl to death? Henriette
is an old lady's name! Let me tell you something, these
Europeans don't trifle with first names, they take them
very seriously. They've got some fine-sounding ones like
Georges, Valéry, François and Jacques. If you'd asked for
my opinion, I'd have given you some sound advice. Not
only did you go and have a baby behind our backs, but
you lumber the poor innocent thing with a name from
the Jurassic period! Do your really think Henriette is a

name for a normal child, eh? You could have called her
Jeanne, for example, or Charlotte, or Odette, or Marie
or I don't know what else, these are fresher names, they
are more attractive and they will guarantee your child
a future ... And then there's another false note, and
I'm not going to hide this from you, it looks to me as
if your daughter will be even darker than her mother,
who is already at the peak of negritude. Anyone would
think you made your baby in a Medieval Christian
oven and left her in there to burn without keeping
an eye on Hell's fire. Because, as you know, normally
when a black child comes into the world he is very pale-
skinned like the children belonging to the Whites, it's
only afterwards that he gradually takes on his original
colour. But your child is already as black as can be. I am
completely taken aback, I've never seen such a charred
baby, not even in Africa!"

Yves the just-Ivorian was grinding his axe about the
colonial debt again:
      "You should have had a mixed-race kid! You haven't
understood the first thing about this country and here
I am declaring until I'm blue in the face that the most
urgent problem facing us lot from the nigger-zone is to
seize here and now the compensation for what we were
made to suffer under colonisation. We should sing along
with the musician Tonton David that we come from a
people who suffered a great deal, from a people who want

to suffer no more. I'm fed up of sweeping the streets of Gaul when I've never seen a White sweeping the streets of my Ivory Coast. Since no one wants to know that we exist in this country, since they pretend not to see us, since we're hired to empty the bins, let us not make things more complicated than they are, the maths is simple, my friend: the more we go out with French women, the more we're leaving our mark on this country so we can say to our former colonisers that we're still here, that they've got to come to an arrangement with us, that tomorrow's world will be packed with negroes at every crossroads, negroes who will be as French as they are, whether they like it or not, that if they don't repay us double-quick for the damages we're seeking, well then we'll go right ahead and bastardise Gaul by all means necessary! You really haven't understood the first thing, you don't listen to me, today you've just proved that the Congolese are the biggest fools on our continent and that they make a lot of noise instead of cutting straight to the chase. Is it with babies like yours that we'll be able to advance our cause, eh? This baby doesn't count in my eyes, it's setting us back a hundred years. What future will it have in a Gaul that will treat it as an immigrant from dawn to dusk? I don't mince my words, now if you don't agree you can do what you like. For me this birth is nothing, it doesn't count! Zero!"

Roger the French-Ivorian was pacing around the pram. He stuck his nose in as if looking for goodness knows what clues. Everybody watched him carry out his inspection. He wheeled the pram over towards the door for more light.

"What on earth's that Roger doing?" asked Paul from the big Congo.

"Is he baptising the little one or something?" wondered Willy.

Roger the French-Ivorian took off my daughter's woollen bonnet to get a better look at her. Then, pulling a face, he stood up again:

"Hold on a minute, Buttologist, this child in question, is it yours?"

"In your opinion, who else would make a child like that here, eh?" Yves the just-Ivorian fired back to his half-compatriot.

The two of them are always feuding, sometimes they go off to fight by the fountain at Les Halles.

Roger the French-Ivorian stood tall, giving a dirty look to his perennial enemy:

"Yves, am I even talking to you? Have you ever shown your child here? I am directing my comments at Buttologist, not you! You do not even exist in my eyes! Go and wait at home for France to pay you compensation for being colonised, as if your own parents hadn't cooperated and benefited from the system! If I were the Minister for Immigration and National Identity in this country, I'd have taken away your resident's card!"

Yves retaliated by insulting his half-compatriot as he walked out of Jip's:

"This White-Negro is starting to get on my nerves! I'm going to have to leave, or things could turn out nastily for him. It's not with half-castes like him that we're going to win the case in this country. While we're busy defending our rights, White-Negroes are auctioning us off the way they did back in the days of slavery. This man will never understand our struggle because he has sold out like all the other half-castes. When the system is anti-Blacks he calls himself White, and when the Whites remind him that a half-caste is just another negro he rejoins the negro crowd! This Roger you see in the bar is French by day and Ivorian by night, never the other way around! I want him to be Ivorian twenty-four hours a day, seven days a week, and for him to stop playing out his little hypocritical game! Sell-out! Pro-slaver brown-nose!"

Roger the French-Ivorian didn't respond to these attacks. It was business as usual.

He turned towards me:

"Aren't you warm-blooded, or what?"

"Why?"

"How can you have a child who doesn't look like you?"

Calmly, I told him to have a good look at my daughter. I took off a shoe to show him my foot.

"Look, we've got the same toes . . ."

"Toes and all that nonsense is for when the grandparents want something to cling on to. We need something concrete, a signature that's authentic and indelible. Are you sure this is your child, eh?"

Just then the little one woke up and started crying. I picked her up to soothe her . . .

Paul gave me several bottles of perfume for Original Colour and tried to cheer me up in a corner:

"Don't listen to that crackpot of a French-Ivorian! It was King Solomon who said that a child is still a child, be he red, yellow or brown. I heard that in a Francis Bebey song. There is also someone who said that woman is the exact place of our birth, and he was right. I can't remember who said it now, but it must have been someone with a brain in his head. People can always argue about the father of a child, there's nothing new there. Take Roger, can he really say that he is his father's son?"

Pierrot the White came over to join us in our corner with the three Pelforts he'd bought me. He put them down on the table:

"Down these three beers for me! One for the Father, one for the Son, and one for the Holy Spirit!"

He reminded me that in the beginning, there wasn't just the Word, but also the verb and the subject and the direct object, and that it was Man in his wickedness who introduced the indirect object. And it was this same wickedness that motivated some of my pals at Jip's. I couldn't make head or tail of his argument, but I found his words comforting compared with what the others had thrown up.

I didn't go back again to Jip's with Henriette. If someone asked me to bring her in, I replied that my baby was not a specimen for some colonial exhibition . . .

still haven't told the Arab on the corner that my ex cleared off to the home country a few months back. I'll have to come clean about it one of these days, I'm going to run out of excuses soon. If I've kept quiet about it until now it's because I know he'll have a heart attack when he finds out.

When I'm opposite him, he's the one who always does the talking, he won't let me get a word in edgeways. Once he's finished with his rant he asks after my ex and my daughter, and I always tell him the same thing: they're on holiday in the Congo. It's like he's delivering the same speech from the day before, he just adds a few new hand gestures here, a few new frowns there. As soon as I walk into his bazaar, I know he'll want to bend my ear for at least twenty minutes' worth. It won't be long now before I need what our neighbour, the young man on the seventh floor, Staircase A, the one whose mother is poorly over towards Champagnac de Belair, calls a "cast-iron alibi". But my tactic is to deal with the problem as it arises. I just can't see myself saying, out of the blue:

"I've been lying every time you asked me for news

about my daughter and my partner, it's been ages now since they left for the home country with that good-for-nothing, the Hybrid."

There's no point in jumping ahead of things, I'm not ready to give the game away. It's a matter of honour, and dignity . . .

From his cash till, our Arab on the corner can see everyone who comes out of our building. His shop isn't actually on the corner but in the middle of the street, right opposite our block. Which means, properly speaking, we should call him the Arab opposite instead of the Arab on the corner. Then again, since the dawn of time, people have always talked about the Arab on the corner, and it's not for me to snap my fingers and start a revolution. I mean, if we decided to question everything that reminds us of how unfair, or even offensive, the French language can be towards certain groups of people, well, we'd never hear the end of it. There would be civil wars in the former territories of the French Empire, and Gaul herself would be torn apart to fall into the hands of the Romans. We would have as many trials as there are dead leaves waiting to be shovelled up. We'd lose all track of who was complaining about what, not to mention the date of this or that injustice. So the Members of the Académie Française would finally have a full-time job on their hands. I'm imagining the prostitutes would be keenest to hold people to account because the French language is a real bitch when it comes to them. They might want to know, for example, why a man with the common touch is a national treasure while a woman with the common touch is a whore? Why is a man with an eye for the ladies a charmer while a lady with an eye for the men is a trollop? Why is a "courtier" someone who is close to power while a "courtisan" is a streetwalker? No, I don't want to fight that battle. People talk about the Arab on the corner, and so do I, even if his shop is opposite our building, while down on the corner there's a locksmith who's your typical Frenchman, except that he hasn't got a beret and a baguette . . .

If you're not in the mood to greet our Arab on the corner, he'll step outside and give you a curt lecture on good manners. Even when you think he's got his back turned and you can dodge him, he manages to lay his hands on you. It's as if he's got a third eye in the back of his neck that's more powerful than the Bible stories about the eye watching Cain. And since, like every Arab on the corner, ours doesn't close shop until very late, about one in the morning, there's no deceiving his lynx's eye. His life is his shop, and vice versa. The kids who steal his bananas from the display stand outside have first-hand experience of this. He doesn't say a word, he just watches and then waits for their parents to show up at his grocery store. And that's when he gives them a

remedial class in bringing up young people today. If
the kids are stealing it's because their parents have failed
to educate them properly. So it's not the children you
should blame, but their mothers and fathers . . .

He eats behind his till, and he reads his old copy of
the Koran there too. I sometimes wonder when he goes
to the toilet. If he's human like us, he must hear the call
of nature at some stage in the day. But no, he's there,
unbudgeable, energetic, everywhere at once, never in
the least bit tired.

The Arab on the corner is bald with a small paunch and
a grey goatee. He's got these thick hairs that have taken
root in his ears and he tugs on them from time to time
when he's talking to you. The local residents can buy
goods on credit at his shop, he has a large exercise book
just for them. The surnames of slow payers are marked
in red. He calls everybody "comrades", and I'm treated
to "my African brother" because according to him Africa
is the land of helping each other out, it's the continent
of solidarity. He maintains that the first man on earth
was African, the other races came later. So all men are
immigrants, except for the Africans who are at home
here down below. And what's more, according to him, we
Africans are Egyptians and we followed the Nile in order
to spread ourselves across the continent. He whispers in
my ear that the West will never be able to teach that fact
because it would call too many things into question:

"For too long the West has force-fed us lies and bloated us with pestilence, my African brother! Do you know which black poet spoke those courageous words, eh? It's not easy telling Europeans that in reality they are nothing but immigrants themselves and that their continent actually belongs to the Africans who were the first men on earth! Take that Senegalese man, for example, a great historian, a great scholar, I've forgotten his name … What was he called again? It's on the tip of my tongue … Well, it will come back to me, and anyway it's easy enough with the Senegalese, there's no point in over-complicating things, they're all called Diop, what matters is finding out their first name. The Senegalese man I'm talking about was so strong, my African brother. When he demonstrated to the Whites, with scientific evidence to the ready, that there were plenty of Blacks in ancient Egypt, and that those Blacks were the masters, well, Europe categorically refused to recognise this. People claimed that the Blacks weren't capable of building the pyramids, that they'd been cursed since the dawn of time when Ham, one of Noah's sons, saw his father naked. The Blacks would therefore be condemned to the curse of Ham with a male organ so oversized that no underpants could ever conceal it. The Senegalese historian fought against these kinds of prejudices. At the Sorbonne, the Whites refused to let him defend his dissertation! Can you, in all good conscience, call that normal behaviour, eh? In your opinion, why does Europe behave in this way towards Africans, eh? Well, let me tell you: if the Europeans conceded that there were Blacks in Egypt, intelligent Blacks, Black leaders, Blacks with regular sized male organs, they would also have to concede that the European philosophers who'd been coming to Egypt since Antiquity did so in order to steal our ideas and go off to develop their own philosophy without so much as a by your leave. And that is why, my African brother, Europe will always tell you that Egypt is not Africa! But everybody knows now that Europe has, for a long time, force-fed us lies and bloated us with pestilence . . ."

*  *  *

I remember that when our daughter was born, the Arab on the corner used to come to our building in person to bring us mineral water, milk and Pampers. I had this idea that he was off-loading damaged stock in the same way that developed countries send their out-of-date medicines to underdeveloped countries. I was wrong and I felt ashamed for doubting the Arab on the corner's generosity. He would knock on our door, stop to talk for a minute or two and treat us to his jokes, which were generally about the Jews and the Arabs. You had to laugh even if you didn't understand them at all. And we would force out big guffaws and sometimes even tears of laughter. It wasn't difficult for my ex because laughing came easily to her. And if I laughed it was because I was laughing at the way she laughed.

The Arab on the corner told us we should waste no time in moving apartments, that it would be hard when the child started moving on all fours. Our little one would break everything in the studio. He said that children like scampering about and poking their noses everywhere in the home. And in a space as cramped as ours, Henriette would feel like a prisoner in a cage. He promised to help us out because some compatriots of his worked for a property agency in Charenton-Le-Pont. But you couldn't mention the banlieue to my ex, even if it was the closest one to Paris. Just hearing the word "banlieue " was enough to make her break out in cold sores . . .

So from time to time we got bottles, milk and nappies for free. I didn't feel comfortable with it, but how could I say no to the Arab on the corner without offending him? We took it all and stored it in a corner of our studio. My ex was happy, but not me. To clear her conscience, she used to say:

"Why let it bother you? It's not like we asked him for anything! He's mainly doing it for our daughter because in the Bible or the Koran the children are the bosses. The Kingdom of Heaven is for them. Plus he knows that by giving to the children God will pay him back many times over, and that's not counting the twenty-two virgins he'll have automatic right to in Paradise as a reward for his upright behaviour on earth."

And I would object:

"We're not the only ones with a child in this neighbourhood! Why doesn't he give to all the familes with children?"

"Look, it's because we live right opposite his bazaar! And anyway, I've seen him giving sweets and bananas to other children . . ."

* * *

Since then, whenever I've walked into his shop on my way back from Jip's, the Arab on the corner gets excited, he holds onto my pack of Pelforts so he can talk to me for longer. He shows me his till, complains that money isn't worth what it used to be in the days of the new franc and the old franc. He curses the big supermarkets for killing off small businesses. He talks to me about his family who stayed behind in his country, about the house he's building over there, about the competition in our neighbourhood with the Pakistanis and the Chinese who aren't cutting him any slack:

"Business isn't what it used to be when I came to this country. Now there are more shopkeepers than customers! That's globalisation for you: Chinese and Pakistanis at the end of every street, what can I say? I swear, my African brother, these Chinese and Pakistanis, they buy up everything! They've got money that turns up from their countries via the sewers of Paris! Did you hear they're setting up shop in that country of yours too, all the way over there? In your opinion what on earth are they going to do in the heart of darkness now that slavery has been abolished and the colonisers have either packed up their bags or else been driven out by the natives, eh? Our new settlers are the Chinese and Pakistanis that you can see in our streets. They are crafty, they say they are different from our former masters and that we all come from developing countries, that we are all the third world, and they pretend to build us palaces of the people so that our parliamentarians can sit in session in leather armchairs with air conditioning and a fountain in the courtyard, is this what is going to put bread on the table for the ordinary people, eh, my African brother? A settler is a settler even if he builds you a great big palace of the people! Now listen, I'm going to explain to you how the Chinese and the Pakistanis arrived in France and settled here by using the antelope tactic: first, they scattered in great numbers, then they gently started to get themselves established, without making any noise, whereas you Blacks and us Arabs when we arrive somewhere the first offence we commit is trouble with the neighbours! The Chinese and the Pakistanis? Those people are crafty! You don't see them on the eight o'clock news burning cars, they don't go out on strike with the other immigrants, they smile at everybody. And that smile is key to their business. If all the illegals in this country smiled I don't think we'd ever see them catching charter flights home, they'd travel back business class with Air France. I swear, my African brother!"

I'm champing at the bit as I listen to him. But he hasn't finished yet.

He's off again, with even more energy than before:

"We woke up one morning as we were opening our shops to find that the Chinese and the Pakistanis were there already and they'd bought everything without taking out a single loan because these people have their own banks. But when I ask for a loan here, it's a whole to-do. The banker as good as wants to see my bicycle licence and ask whether I eat with my fingers or a fork! And the result is: my sort of business hardly exists in the neighbourhood any more. We are the last Mohicans. No more Arab on the corner, it's over! Even my small business here, well, I've had enough, it will end up in the hands of the Chinese and the Pakistanis. But we are the kind of people who sacrifice ourselves for others. There's no denying the fact that we're a public service. When I sell my merchandise, I don't see the colour of my customers' skin. I sell to the poor, and I sell to the rich, I sell to the handicapped, I sell to the Blacks, I sell to the Arabs, I sell to all the races that exist down here below because whatever race we may be, we all have red blood . . ."

He falls silent. I can almost see the tears in his eyes. He turns away from me as if to hide them.

And then he straightens himself up, he stares at me and off he goes again:

"My African brother, this is a serious situation, we all need to help each other out here. This country wouldn't exist if it weren't for us, do you get my gist, eh? We have always been there each time France was at war even though we could have stayed at home. But have the Pakistanis and the Chinese helped France? Have they shed their blood for this country? The day when we Arabs on the corner aren't here any more, this country will lose everything, and I mean everything. France will lose her Arabs on the corner! Are you getting my gist? And you Blacks too, my African brothers, be vigilant, because after us, it will be your turn! They say there are too many people working on the black market, have you heard that? So if you all leave this country, it's true there won't be any more Blacks, but there won't be any work either. Enough is enough, I say. They shout at us on the telly, on the radio and in the newspapers, but are we the ones digging the hole in the social? We still have one thing, my African brother, and that is the African Union, this is the only way we will build the African Unity of the Enlightened Guide, Muammar Gaddafi!"

He says all that while holding onto my pack of Pelforts. I cough to let him know I've got to go home now, and he starts up again:

"Wait, hold on a minute, my African brother, I have something very important to tell you because this world is falling apart before our very eyes, and we're doing nothing about it. And I'm not even talking about the hole in the social that's as big as you like, I'm just talking about what I can see before me, in this street, in front of your building. I'm sixty-three and a half years old, I grew up with the strictest respect for my parents, but also for strangers, and I'm proud of that. Respect forms the basis of society, are you still getting my gist, my African brother? Do you know what France's great problem is? Well, I'm going to tell you what the real problem is for France. Don't listen to what they say on the telly, it's just meant to confuse us. France's problem lies elsewhere, it is deep, it is in the morals. Even the unemployment is not it, even the hole in the social is not it, France's problem it is RESPECT! It is a legacy, a very important legacy, RESPECT. But the youth of today, what do they do, eh? Well let me tell you, they break everything! They think that they are smarter than their parents! So they talk when their parents are talking. They bring their girlfriends or boyfriends home with them to go jiggy-jiggy in their bedrooms when in my day we hid in the sewers for that. And they do that thing in full view of their family. They don't even go to school any more, they don't read even the Koran any more, are you getting my gist? I ask you! And as for the girls? It is complete mayhem, and their parents are guilty for letting them wear mini-skirts, jeans with holes on the butts, red thongs and dragon tattoos, as well as T-shirts with their breasts for all to see! How are the rascals not supposed to rape them, eh? It's not the rapists' fault, it's the girls displaying their merchandise who are to blame. When you go walking with a bone in the street, the dogs in the neighbourhood will chase after it, I swear to you! But when you put that bone in the bottom of your basket, the neighbourhood dogs don't know about the bone, and that is the end of the matter. Now, I realise that dogs can also smell there's a bone hidden somewhere, because, don't believe it, my African brother, French dogs aren't as stupid as you'd think, they've also got a very strong nose like the African dogs. But me, I've never seen a dog of any nationality whatsoever opening the bag of a normal woman to take out a bone hidden in there. And when I see these weird girls passing by in front of my shop – and some of them even come here to provoke me – I think to myself the world is going to the dogs, big time, I swear, my African brother. And whose fault is all this? Can you answer me that, eh? IT'S THE FAULT OF THE WEST! Do you call it civilisation, what we're seeing in this country? Do you call it development, what we're seeing in this country? I'd rather my country remained under-developed until the end of time, provided it doesn't follow this path, you do get my gist, don't you . . . ?"

I nod while wondering when he'll finally bring his rant to an end.

"Today, it's on me," he declares. "The bottles of Pelfort are a gift from me, and so are these bananas, my brother, we are all Africans together!"

"Thanks very much . . ."

"How are your wife and your daughter? Still on holiday in the home country?"

"Still there, yes."

"Lucky them. With this shitty weather we're having, if I were in their shoes I'd stay in the sun for a long time . . . She's a real go-getter, your wife! Very brave, very obedient, always working or looking after your little one!"

"Thank you . . ."

**I** **must get used** to the idea that Original Colour is back in the home country with the Hybrid who plays the tom-toms in a group nobody's ever heard of here, but from what I hear it's a hot ticket over there and normal girls have fainting fits during its shitty live gigs as if they were at a James Brown concert.

Do people from the home country know what real music is? All they do is writhe, go into a trance as soon as the drum beat starts. Is playing the tom-toms in a group a respectable activity, eh? Can you come home at the end of the day and say to your woman, honey, I play the tom-toms, that's my job and here are my payslips? Is that what's going to fill the hole in the social and take the brakes off social mobility? And to think that Roger the French-Ivorian wants me to write about the tom-toms or drums in my diary. I ask you! The tom-toms are for people who like a night-time racket, end of story. That's why, unlike the Arab on the corner, I have respect for the Chinese and the Pakistanis. They're decent guys who've unfairly got a bad reputation for working like dogs and never saying a word when they're not harming anyone. At least they don't play the tom-

toms in this country. The day someone invents silent tom-toms, a lot of old negroes will lose their reason for living. The tom-tom is something we should get rid of for good because its time is up. In the past they used to have fun sounding this instrument in the cotton fields of the American South to tell the other slaves watch out the master's coming with his dogs, make it look like you're working or else he's going to whip you or sell you to another master who's even more wicked and who'll chop the legs off any slave who makes a run for it. It was also with their tom-toms that these slaves wept for the faraway suns of the black continent when they had the blues. And it was also with the tom-toms that the Africans greeted the suns of independence, but what they didn't know was that they'd find themselves going from Scylla to Charybdis. Now is no longer a time for having fun and working in the cotton fields, now is no longer the dawn of independence, but we beat those tom-toms from morning to night, to the point of leading happily settled women astray . . .

\* \* \*

Of course, I could always have gone for the Hybrid, sent a few friends his way who would have rearranged his face back in the home country. But what good would that have done? I'm not a man who enjoys trouble. I'm polite and, unlike Mr Hippocratic, I'm very sociable, I'm open to all sorts of debate and I'm conscious of the way our society of the spectacle is evolving. I am familiar with the ways of the world. But not with fighting and conflict. I don't like arguments and disputes. In fact, when a fight breaks out among the guys from the banlieues at the Gare du Nord or métro Marcadet-Poissonniers, I don't separate the fighters, I distance myself from the battlefield, I let the belligerents fix up their self-portraits the way they want to. You should never disturb contemporary artists, just leave them to express the madness of their art when they paint their *Guernica*. Let them fight according to their rules, I'm not going to play at being referee. Fighting often amounts to a lack of communication, by which I mean ignorance about the ways of the world.

So when there is an argument or a fight I take off because just one word from a bystander, and they stop arguing or waging war, and turn on you instead, as it says in one of La Fontaine's fables, your ears will be mistaken for the horns of the animal that wounded the Lion and you will endure the wrath of the king of beasts. It's thanks to my extreme cautiousness that my criminal record is still clean, and it's not everybody who has a record like mine. It's so clean they could use it when they're short on forms at the ministry of justice. Not only that but I don't hang out with delinquents, I don't keep company with criminals, I don't know any judges and I've never sat opposite a lawyer . . .

That Congolese minstrel doesn't even come up to my ankles, he doesn't even come up to my Achilles' heel.

Has he got a moustache like me or like my friend the writer Louis-Philippe? Has he ever worn Weston shoes in his life? Does he know how to knot a silk tie? Does he know why some shirt collars have three buttons? Could he recognise one hundred per cent lambswool? Does he own a Francesco Smalto suit with a topstitched lining? Has he ever seen the film *Three The Hard Way* with Jim Kelly, Jim Brown and Fred Williamson? Has he ever read *The Dirty Havana Trilogy* by Juan Pedro Guttiériez ? NO, NO AND NO AGAIN!

I've got to calm down here or I might end up punching my typewriter. I've got to remember that the Hybrid is short even when he's standing up. Plus he's got one eye bigger than the other, and his calloused hands look like the claws of a crab from the Côte Sauvage at Pointe-Noire who can't decide whether to go back into the sea or to scuttle across the sand. His head is like a rectangular parallelepiped. His skin is like very dark laterite, and if you take a good look there's no difference between him and those famous sculptures of fighters that the Senegalese artist Ousmane Sow exhibited on the Pont des Arts, and which frightened some Parisians so much that the poor things were forced to cross the Seine using different bridges where joy wouldn't come again after each sorrow . . .

Original Colour will be sorry one day. When you're lucky enough to have a guy like me you don't leave him, you hold on to him.

Sometimes I wonder what people are looking for

in life. What on earth is she going to do with the Hybrid, eh? Listen to the tom-toms night and day? Tag along behind for his concerts in the back of beyond? What is this business of restoring drumming to the poor Africans of Africa? These days the Africans over there don't give a monkey's about traditional African drumming, because it's something they've left to the Whites who take lessons in it, who dress up in African textiles to look the part and who are rather pleased with themselves because they reckon they're doing their bit for integration and cross-cultural exchange. I can understand a White learning to play the tom-toms, it makes him look cool, the kind of guy who is open to all the cultures of the world and who is not in the least bit racist. But a Black who plays the tom-toms is dodgy, it's too much about returning to his roots, to the beginning, to the natural state, about having a sense of rhythm. It's not for nothing that the Europeans are so interested in African drumming. It's because they want to find out how things worked where we came from, when it was the only means of communication.

* * *

The Hybrid didn't know how to make the most of his instrument in the current circumstances. If I were a drummer like him, well, I'd have gone for the easy ride, I'd have stayed in Europe to cash in while the going was good, I'd have played bum notes for workers in the sticks, at nurseries in the banlieues, at the after-school clubs in the 13th arrondissement, at the Porte de Vincennes fair, at the old people's homes in Rueil Malmaison, in prisons and psychiatric asylums, because music knows no barriers. There's money to be made because I've noticed that Whites go easy on our music, especially where those shitty tom-toms are involved. It all gets more complicated when fantasist negroes add in a bit of piano here, a bit of violin there. How are Whites supposed to deal with that, eh? They think to themselves: "Hold on, hold on a minute, your hullaballoo is fine by us but don't reduce our Bach and our Mozart to this rudimentary level!"

They're not wrong, when it comes to their music it's written down, you read it, you go to school to learn how to do it, you even have to repeat the year if you're stupid. But we've still got the kind of music that's in our bones and gets handed down from generation to generation. Bullshit! Rubbish! Go to music school just like everybody else, end of story. And on the day of the final exam it will be plain for everyone to see that this business about the music getting under our skin is just claptrap because the Whites have skin too even if unfortunately for them it's not black like ours . . .

The Hybrid didn't sense the winds of change. He thinks the Berlin Wall is still standing, that General de Gaulle will spring to life and bring back our prophet André

Grenard Matsoua to Maya-Maya airport in Brazzaville. He is convinced that Nelson Mandela is still in prison, and that Diego Maradona will play in the next World Cup. It's only to be expected, I have no idea what his intelligence quota is. Like the ostrich, his eye is bigger than his brain.

When I imagine my daughter calling him "papa" it makes my nose run but I refuse to blow it because I want to stay snotty on the subject of Original Colour and the Hybrid. Nothing can curb my desire to express myself, to write in this diary what I feel about him deep down

. . .

The Hybrid was becoming more and more of an intruder in our lives. Whenever his group had a concert in Paris, he would turn up at our place with no notice but lots of presents for the little one. He would lean over our daughter, rock her as if she were his own, and talk to her in a strange dialect. And since the Arab on the corner had explained to me that children can understand all the languages in the world, I wondered what that minstrel was telling Henriette. He would talk quickly with a smile that stretched all the way to his ears. And the child would fidget, giggle, hold out her arms to him. At which point the Hybrid would take a teddy bear out of his bag, followed by a doll, followed by a pink dress.

Was it thanks to the wild imaginings of Roger the French-Ivorian that all of a sudden I too found my daughter didn't look like me? The more I thought about it, the more it occurred to me that she looked a bit like the Hybrid. So I would glance from Henriette to the Hybrid and back again: same nose, same eyes, same mouth, the toes were the only body part I could claim.

"There is something I don't understand," I said to

Original Colour, "I am finding that my child here is starting to look too much like your cousin! He has got to stop turning up to show his face to her, I don't want the little one turning out ugly given that I'm handsome!"

Her reply was head-on:

"Have you got a problem with my cousin or what? You do know that he can throw you out of here? You do know that he is the one who paid the deposit on this studio, eh?"

So the Hybrid ended up making me look like the worst kind of miser in Original Colour's eyes. For her he bought shoes, watches, brightly coloured fabrics, trinkets and clingy trousers that squeezed the Side B of my ex even more tightly and drove me to distraction when she refused with increasing regularity to let me stroke even her left toe or her right toe. At one o'clock in the morning I had to negotiate, argue, talk it through, and generally wheedle to the point where it disturbed Mr Hippocratic who could hear me grumbling when she pushed me away, swearing that she wouldn't let me touch her until I changed my attitude towards her cousin.

After the Hybrid went back to Amiens, he used to call Original Colour every evening, wanting to know Henriette's latest news. But I was the one who got shouted at when the phone bill arrived, even though it was those two who spent hours and hours chatting and giggling about nothing.

It's true that I frequently called Louis-Philippe, but we never talked for longer than ten or fifteen minutes. I kept him up to date with my writings, and told him about the birds I'd seen in the trees in the park, I assured him that I'd noted down their tiniest movements, their briefest songs, and he promised that he would read my work, and that he'd give me his opinion. When I wanted to confide in him about what was going on at home, I went to pay him a visit, we'd sit at a café table in his neighbourhood and I would read out what I'd scribbled down over the previous days and about how the Hybrid was wreaking havoc on our relationship . . .

\* \* \*

It was at Bar Sangho, in Château Rouge, that I first met the person nicknamed Carcass. Perhaps it's partly down to what he told me that Original Colour and I have come to this point.

That day I'd bought a round of Pelforts for two compatriots who had arranged to meet me at Bar Sangho. A third compatriot sat down with us and insisted on me buying him a Pelfort too, even though he'd got a nerve, we hardly knew each other. He claimed we had a connection, saying that his father and mine used to be great friends. I wracked my brains and realised he was right, but that it was his big brother, Hervé, who I used to know when I was at the Lycée Karl Marx. So Carcass was mistaking me for my little brother. I bought him a Pelfort. He told me he was a musician in a traditional group, that things hadn't worked out for him, that he'd been given the boot from one day to the next by someone called Mitori.

That name rang a bell. It took me a while before I realised it was the Hybrid's real name. Lucien Mitori . . .

Half an hour later, Carcass had already got through four bottles of beer. As soon as he raised a hand in the direction of the counter, he got served as if he was the one footing the bill.

He started raving, he kept on calling me "big brother", and telling me I wasn't just anybody:

"Big brother, you are a powerful man! Eeeeh! You are really somebody! There are some shady characters in Paris, but you are not one, big brother. You see that suit you're wearing? It's a terrific suit! Back home you would catch the girls like flies, I swear to you! Outfits like that, not even the Whites know where they're sold or how they're made. I'm telling you, big brother, I'm trying to get by the best I can, I'm a true musician, me! There aren't two musicians of my calibre in all of Paris. I'm telling you! I have recorded with artists like Lokua Kanza, Ray Lema and Richard Bona. I nearly recorded with old Manu Dibango, but it fell through at the last minute because his schedule was too full. So I play here and there, but it's tough. Last month I was still playing with Griots Of The Congo. They didn't want me in that group because I've got talent. My time

will come, I swear to you, big brother! In your view,
why did they kick me out of Griots Of The Congo, eh?
There was a coup staged against me. And it was Mitori
who mounted that coup d'état because I was starting to
have too much power and success in the group, because
I was nearly number two. He was scared that one day
I'd be the boss, and most of all he was scared that I
wasn't from the same ethnic group as him. Is that any
kind of a way to behave, big brother? I don't like that
Mitori! He's a dog! He's a hypocrite! I'd had enough.
Our people will never change!"

He turned round, saw the waitress walking past and
grabbed hold of her:

"What are you doing wiggling your backside around
my big brother like that? Do you want to make his head
spin or something? Do you think it's a fashion show
here? Can't you see my bottles are empty and my big
brother is looking after me properly? So what are you
waiting for when you could replace them double quick,
eh?"

I signalled to him to calm down.

"No, big brother, I don't understand these African
bars any more. With the Whites, when a bottle is empty,
it is empty! Another one is brought, double-quick! But
with us, the waitresses go round in circles and flirt with
the customers. Listen up, girl, bring me two ice-cold
Pelforts and leave my big brother in peace!"

The waitress went off to sulk at the back of the bar.

Carcass moved his chair closer to mine:

"Big brother, thank you for these beers, you are not just anybody! Do you realise that the Congolese here in France form musical groups based on ethnic lines, as if we were still in the home country? Is that what they call promoting the traditional music of our nation? What image are we projecting of ourselves in Europe, eh? They tell everybody they're playing music from the Congo, but what about me, aren't I Congolese too? It's because I'm not from their ethnic group that they've excluded me. He's a dog, that Mitori! He's a hypocrite, that Mitori! I don't like him one little bit, that Mitori! When he is sweating he stinks. He is short as the dwarves you see with Snow White in those picture books for European kids. And another thing, when he plays the tom-toms his instrument is taller than he is. Have you ever seen that before, eh, a man shorter than his own drum? If I run into him, I will break his nose! At some of our concerts he would take me to one side, and say that the producers didn't have any money and we had to reduce the numbers. Big brother, you've known this country for a long time like me, have you ever seen a white producer who doesn't have money, eh? Or else, how come your Michel Sardous and your Charles Aznavours are never bankcrupt, eh? All the white producers have always got money, and I won't let anyone bullshit on the subject. It's the black producers who don't have anything, and that's all there is to it.

They rob the artists, they run off with the cashbox back to the home country, and that's why we don't have musicians who are as rich as your Michel Sardous and your Charles Aznavours. Big brother, name me a single one of our musicians who is rich. Nothing! Zero! They live poor, they die poor, the worst is their music gets forgotten too if there isn't a White taking care of it. I'm not being extremist when I say that, and these Pelforts aren't turning my brain in the direction of Mecca. Having a white producer is an opportunity to get rich. But that Mitori, he just wanted to get rich by himself, and he wanted to let the people from his ethnic group profit out of it. So he hired another conga player instead of me, a guy from the village where he was born, when I was the one who trained that musician here in Paris! Do you see the problem? What am I in this story, eh? What experience does he have, this Mitori, to run a group in France, eh? Me, I can play the tom-toms better than him! He is just a small-time thug, a no one, an anarchist as they say in France. He came to Nancy thanks to his cousin who then kicked him out because he was a slacker, because he wanted to do the business with the woman of his good Samaritan cousin, but the woman said NO, NO, NO, NO, NO!"

Madame Sangho, the bar owner, came over to tell him to lower his voice, that there were other customers who were disturbed by the noise we were making.

"Who are these customers? What do they have over

my big brother? Leave me in peace, woman! I need to talk! I've had enough! Am I looking for trouble in this bar? My big brother is buying my beers, he has got money, he is well dressed, have you seen his suit? Do you know where he bought it? Are we in France or are we not? The customer is king!"

Then, leaning over as if he didn't want the other compatriots to share what he was about to confide in me, he whispered in a deep voice:

"Big brother, I am going to tell you something you must keep to yourself . . . It is very serious what that Mitori has done. He's a bastard! It's because you don't know him, big brother! If you come across him here or anywhere, whatever you do don't offer him a beer because I can see you're too kind and you'll always be taken for a bloody fool. You're too nice, and too much of a bloody fool. Mitori is a crook, he's a snake, I swear! I won't tell you what a scandal there was over in Nancy where he lived before! That was where he took the virginity of the daughter of a lawyer from back home who dabbles in politics and who wants to become president by the way with a little help from the Americans. Do you think the Americans will help a guy like that who didn't fight in the Vietnam War and who didn't bomb the Iraqis? The Americans only respect you if you have fought by their side in war. But we Congolese, have we been in battle alongside the Americans? NO, NO, NO! This lawyer had Mitori locked up for two years, the story was reported in the newspapers because the daughter of that lawyer was only seventeen but Mitori had been an adult for a long time, and the French don't mess around when it comes to that kind of thing. Back home, seventeen isn't a problem, you can already have two children by then, or even three or four, but that doesn't happen here, you're locked up if you lay a finger on a girl that young. When Mitori came out of prison, he went into hiding in Amiens and never set foot in Nancy again. I know everything, that's why he's scared of me, that's why he's kicked me out of the group. And the girl in question, whose virginity he took, I mean the lawyer's daughter, she's not even beautiful! Not beautiful at all! Ugly as a louse! If you saw her, you would think to yourself how can a girl be as ugly as that? It's true she's got a great ass, and I wouldn't say no, if she was offering. I'd close my eyes and do the business without leaving any marks, but I mean really is it because of that kind of girl that me, Carcass, would go to prison for two years, eh? Let's not get carried away here. And another thing, this girl I am talking about she is so black you can only see her eyes and her teeth!"

I was sweating profusely, and I was thinking hard, I wasn't listening to him. I wanted to go home, I knew I wouldn't do anything or say anything to Original Colour.

I paid the bill and left some money for Carcass

because he wanted to stay a while longer. He tore a strip of paper out of his notebook and scrawled down a telephone number. I told him I didn't have a number, that I would call him. I didn't want him to get Original Colour when he called me.

"Thank you, big brother, you are really somebody! . . ."

* * *

A week later, I called Carcass. He seemed very worked up about something:

"Big brother! I've been waiting on your call for days! Why didn't you ring me, eh? Guess what, yesterday I spotted Mitori, he was with that very black and very ugly girl I was telling you about, I mean the daughter of the lawyer in Nancy. They were in Château Rouge, at Pauline Nzongo's restaurant. And there was me thinking their story was over!"

Like a fool, I'd been looking after our daughter that evening while those two cousins were out eating and getting drunk at a Congolese restaurant on Rue de Suez

. . .

One time the Hybrid stayed in Paris for over a month even though his group didn't have any concerts booked. It's true he didn't sleep at ours, but I noticed Original Colour losing her head during that period, she was always getting dressed up, spending more and more time away from home and coming back very late. My cousin this, my cousin that. I won't be back early tonight, don't wait up for me. Pick up the kid from the Cape Verdean childminder and feed her at seven o'clock on the dot . . .

That same month I thought I was going to explode when I found the Hybrid sitting comfortably in our only armchair. This armchair was my place, I was the one who had bought it, and I sat in it to watch my programmes about those couples who go to an island to resist the temptations of handsome men and beautiful women. The Hybrid was holding the remote and watching *The Young and The Restless*. My daughter was fast asleep, and he was shedding a tear in front of the telly because of his soap involving a love story and an inheritance, as well as poisonings every two minutes and trite dialogue. All he was wearing was a pair of shorts, he was gobbling up my garlic saucisson with some cassava and a hot pepper, and drinking my beers that I'd bought from the Arab on the corner. He was surrounded by empty bottles.

I asked him what the hell he was doing in the capital instead of being with his fellow musicians in their remote corner of northern France. He replied that the whole group was in Paris to record a CD, and that he and the others had decided to go back to the home country for good. In the meantime, he was making the most of it by looking after Henriette while Original Colour was at work. All in all, he was helping his cousin and I should be grateful to him.

At this rate he was as good as living with us. How can you stay round at other people's from morning to midnight? According to Original Colour, the cousin was doing a good job of looking after the little one. I'll admit that when he used to sing things to our little girl, she held out her arms to him and burst out laughing. She was getting so used to him that when I wanted to hold her and sing her the things from here that people sing to little French children – things like *Marlborough Has Left for the War* and *There's Some Tobacco in My Snuffbox* – she would blub as if she'd been stung by a red ant, she wanted to stay in the Hybrid's arms and she would only listen to the songs from back home. This pleased him no end, I tell you he was taunting me . . .

I had really had enough by the end. But I couldn't say this out loud. Original Colour kept praising the minstrel's talents, which encouraged him to leave two of his drums round at ours on the grounds that Henriette loved the sound of our ancestral instrument. On Sunday afternoons he would make a bloody awful racket, giving me a migraine and making Mr Hippocratic bellow that we should go back to the bush we came from and take our accursed tom-toms with us.

"The Negroes say fuck you!" crowed Original Colour.

* * *

Since the Hybrid felt at home, this meant I was in the way, and Original Colour made this very clear to me. One afternoon I even came back to find the minstrel in my Marithé & François Girbaud T-shirt. He was making a big show of wearing it, and was stretched out on the bed with a Pelfort and the telly tuned to his soap involving love, beauty, glory, inheritance and trite dialogue.

This time, he really had overstepped the limits of hospitality even if it wasn't me who paid the deposit on the studio. Have I lived but to know this infamy? I muttered, through Corneillean gritted teeth.

I vented my anger on him. He defended himself saying it was Original Colour who had lent him my T-shirt, otherwise he would never have taken the liberty of wearing it. And anyway, he added, this top looks like a floorcloth, there are holes everywhere, you can't wear it outside the apartment. Did he follow fashion, this man? To say that about an item of designer clothing by Marithé & François Girbaud! What sacrilege! What ignorance! We nearly came to blows.

"Take that T-shirt off and fast!" I shouted.

He got up, his eyes went red, I could sense the anger rising in his chest. He warned me that if I laid a finger on him he would make mincemeat of me because he had been given a grigri at birth and if he head-butted me I would be out cold for twenty-four and a half hours:

"If you lay a finger on me, I'll send you off to Accident and Emergency in Lariboisière with one head butt! I'm not looking for trouble here. I haven't been in a fight for a long time, but if you want to test the force of my grigri from the village of Tsiaki, then just try touching a single hair on my head!"

On the basis that I didn't want to be out cold for twenty-four and a half hours and end up in A&E in Lariboisière, and because I know that you don't mess around with grigris from Tsiaki, I calmly repeated my request for him to take off my clothes and to pick up his shitty belongings, before finishing off with:

"That T-shirt is mine, it cost an arse and a leg, and we're not talking any old arse here, not even a piece of Original Colour's butt!"

\* \* \*

Later on that same evening, before running to catch the last métro, the Hybrid told his cousin every word I'd said, and she wouldn't let it drop all night.

"You criticised my butt in front of my cousin? Who do you think you are? These buttocks of mine that you're insulting, aren't they the same ones that turned your head that first day in front of Soul Fashion, eh? Have you ever seen any others like these in all your life? Do you know how many people would pay to have me? Do you look at yourself in the mirror before you start talking to people? I am asking you again: who do you think you are, eh? You do nothing in this house, you go drinking with the riff-raff at Jip's, you work part-time, and you think you can play the boss round at my place?"

The Hybrid never did come back to our apartment and Original Colour stopped talking to me. At least, I thought to myself, we've got rid of the minstrel. But we still had two of his drums at home, and they got up my nose. When I looked at those instruments it was as if the cousin was there and our ancestors were talking to me, or even mocking me.

"So when is he going to pick up his things, that cousin of yours? We don't have any space in this studio as it is!"

This question was the last straw. Original Colour turned into a wounded tigress:

"Enough is enough! Enough is enough! Enough is

enough! If you won't leave this studio then I'm the one who is walking out!"

She was roaring so loudly that Mr Hippocratic banged on the wall several times.

"Silence, you Congolese negroes, or I'll call the police!"

I never did the business with her again after that. I took to sleeping on the floor, and eating out with my pals from Jip's. I spent time with Louis-Philippe who kept saying to me:

"Write, write about what you're feeling . . ."

I'd never taken my hat off for anybody before. If I found myself eating humble pie now, it was for the sake of my child's education so that one day she would turn out a dutiful daughter. I was trying to get on top of things, to dilute my palm wine with water, and not to think about what Carcass had told me at Bar Sangho, I even stopped calling him so I wouldn't have to suffer any more. I wanted to become a responsible man, I wanted to show Original Colour that I didn't give a monkey's about her history with the Hybrid when she was seventeen.

So I only went to the park once or twice with my typewriter, even though there were flocks of birds hopping about in the branches and waiting just for me.

When I made it to Jip's I only stayed for two hours tops, I downed two or three Pelforts and let my thoughts roam free. I was picturing the Hybrid with Original Colour a few years earlier when he was taking her somewhere, maybe to a barn to do the business. The poor girl was fragile, maybe she didn't think she was ready to enter the world of adults, or else she did want it, to free herself at last from her parents, and above all from that lawyer. Back then, the Hybrid must have been even shorter and he already had sweaty armpits. And then, bam! he forced things. According to Paul from the big Congo, who used to drink by my side in those times of great confusion, a girl never forgets her first man. Hey presto, I would drink another beer, and erase those images. I would catch the métro to Etienne Marcel in order to get back to north Paris, hoping that the Hybrid hadn't returned to settle down in front of the telly and watch his stories about love, inheritance, glory and beauty . . .

Paul from the big Congo picked up straight away that the sparks were flying at home:

"You can always talk to me, Buttologist, you know how discreet I am. I mean have you ever heard me making fun of you the way the others do here? I'm getting more and more worried about you because you are not the man I used to know, anyone would think you don't sleep any more. You come here, you only have two or three Pelforts and then you run back home, it is like you've been given a set time and you can't be late, not even by a second. Is it Original Colour who is making your life a misery?"

I told him that everything was fine, that I was just a bit tired.

"Look me in the eye . . . You are lying . . . Yes, you are lying. I can see that your eyes are all red. You're not going to tell me it's because of those stories you write on your typewriter! What is wrong?"

* * *

I found out that the Hybrid had been talking to our Arab on the corner and that the shopkeeper had enjoyed his company.

One evening when I went into his shop to buy some Pelforts and milk he said to me:

"For too long the West has force-fed us lies and bloated us with pestilence! Do you know which black poet spoke those courageous words, eh? My African brother, last night I was with your relative, I mean the cousin of your wife, so he is your cousin too. I often used to see him coming out of your building very late and running in the direction of the métro like the people who steal my vegetables from outside. I was puzzled as to who he was because you might not think it, but I know just about everybody who lives in that building of yours. There is a total of only three Blacks: your woman, your daughter and you. I'm not counting the Caribbean gentleman because he's a case apart, a strange character who does not think he's black, or that there's anything African about him, and that he's French through and through. But as for your cousin there, what a fine fellow! He talks softly, and when he listens he folds his arms and nods with each word. Wouldn't you call that a sign of respect? He is a very educated kind of man because education begins with listening even though in the West they think it all starts with the spoken word. My father, he often used to say to me: 'Djamal, he who listens is wiser than he who speaks . . .' Do you get my gist? Did you realise that cousin of yours there has already been to Algeria and Morocco for some traditional African music concerts? Do you know any African brothers who have worked such wonders? We should be developing exchanges like that between the Maghreb and Black Africa! We are strangers to one another, which is why there are fools who claim that in the old days the Arabs forced their black African brothers into slavery. Can you believe lies like that? Do I have the face of someone whose ancestors were slavers? We need to look into this subject, it is not for nothing that the West didn't dwell on it. It is a sensitive topic. But I say to Westerners that slavery is the West's story, it is not about us Arabs. We are all brothers and no one forces their own brothers into slavery . . . Anyway, all this is to say how happy I was when your cousin told me that he has been to Algeria and Morocco and that he liked these countries! He at least knows how we live over there. He has seen the meaning of respect where we come from. He told me that he wants to convert to Islam, isn't that a good piece of news? He has understood everything, he wants to follow in the footsteps of those Blacks who have become Muslims, those Blacks who have changed and who continue to change the world:

Mohammed Ali, Malcolm X, Karim Abdoul-Jabbar, Louis Farrakhan, etc. Do you realise that your cousin calls me 'papa', eh? I had tears in my eyes! Why haven't you ever called me 'papa' when we've known each other for a long time and I could be your father too given that I am bald and going grey on the sides? If we had a million immigrants like your cousin in this country, we would be strong in the face of the West. And another thing, he has an extraordinary talent, he is the leader of a traditional music group. That group is very well known! Because, between you and me, to go and play in Algeria and Morocco you already have to be very well known throughout the world otherwise the Algerians and the Moroccans will never come to your concert, I know my people. Your cousin also told me that he is going to return to the home country for good with his group. Don't you think that's a respectable attitude? We should all go back home so that one day the African Unity of the Guide Muammar Gaddafi may turn into a reality. The Guide also said, like the pastor Luther King: 'I have a dream'! It is up to us to make his dream come true, it is not the people from the West who are going to give us a leg-up, they are too cunning, they have created their European Community even if they don't get on among themselves. Do you know why they don't get on among themselves? It is because the English don't want anything to do with their single currency. It is because the Danes and the Swedes don't trust it, now look if they really do want that currency then why are they going round in circles instead of jumping on the bandwagon with the other countries, eh? And then, my African brother, why doesn't this Community of theirs accept that Turkey has a place in it, eh? Well, let me tell you, it is because when you see Turkey on the map, this country shares her life between Europe and Asia, and yet the problem it is that the Europeans who had the idea for their Community in the first place are all against polygamy! What are the poor Turks going to do? Move their country? But with our Community that we are going to create thanks to the Guide Gaddafi, if Turkey wants to stay polygamous, well then she will be able to join us, we will open our doors to her because polygamy isn't a problem for us, why it's even enriching! And this is what I was saying to that cousin of yours, and he understood everything from A to Z. He is so modest that he didn't want to tell me he is a great artist who is the pride and joy of our continent. It was only when I asked him where that drumming sound comes from I've been hearing in your building recently, that he told me he was playing the drums to soothe your little one and to help her acclimatise to the African environment! Splendid, don't you think?"

The day Original Colour came back home with a new hairstyle I nearly had a cardiac arrest. She was sporting green and white braids with cowrie shells like the ones Venus and Serena Williams wore when then played at Roland Garros. Her hairstyle wasn't just ridiculous, it showed how stupid and blind I had been despite Carcass indirectly doing me a favour at Bar Sangho.

"Did you go to the hairdresser's in order to charm your cousin?" I asked Original Colour:

"Why?"

"Because you've got to be beautiful for his concert this weekend!"

"I didn't speak to you, I am not speaking to you any more! Leave me alone! Haven't I've got the right to braid my hair the way I like? Is my head your head?"

"Where did you get the money?"

"It was Nicole . . ."

"Nicole?"

"She agreed to let me pay her back when I've got some cash."

Nicole is a good woman. I know her. I owe her respect. She does a great job of running her four hair salons in

Château d'Eau. She decided to go into that line of business ages ago when she was still a medical student. But none of this stopped my male pride from taking an uppercut.

That Saturday I got drunk on Barbancourt rum over at Louis-Philippe the writer's and then I decided to go for a stroll around Château Rouge.

Soul Fashion did its main turnover at the weekend, the shop was always full from morning to night, but the boss had given Original Colour Saturdays off since the little one was born. She mostly stayed at home. This time, though, she was in a rush to go out. She got the kid's bottle ready and wrote on a scrap of paper: "Henriette must have her bottle at seven o'clock on the dot."

She gazed at her reflection for the umpteenth time and left without speaking to me.

I let an hour go by and then I went to drop off Henriette a few metres from our Arab on the corner, with the Cape Verdean mama who was overflowing with kindness to the point of giving us food even though she had seven mouths under her roof to feed. You'd think she was cooking for a whole tribe. She took the little one and asked where Original Colour had gone. I said I was off to meet her in Château-Rouge where we had an appointment.

"Are you sure you're all right, my son?" she pressed me.

"Yes, everything is fine, mama . . ."

* * *

Louis-Philippe's rum was too strong. He said it was because I'd gone over the top with the sugar. After leaving his apartment I walked to Château Rouge with my eyes fixed on the ground because I could barely find my centre of gravity. When I looked up, I thought the sky was going to cave in on me.

I went into Exotic Music, a shop run by a friend who sells music from back home. He was showing me the latest stuff from the big Congo even though I always went there to listen to albums from the seventies and eighties. He played "Liberté" by Franco Luambo Makiadi from Tout-Puissant OK Jazz. The song moved me, I was seeing the country again, that concert by the illustrious musician at the Joli Soir in Pointe Noire. We were under-age at the time, and the doormen wouldn't let us. We had to slip them something. But I didn't have anything. So I climbed a mango tree and held onto a branch to get a view of the great Franco with his paunch and his guitar, which he strummed like a virtuoso. I wanted to grow up big and fat like him, to play the guitar like him, to wiggle like him. I admired his musicians who wore silk shirts and clingy trousers. I couldn't keep my eyes off the couples taking over the dance floor. They were sweating, the men squeezed their partners tight, those without a partner waited in a corner, looking as sad as a dog with an ungrateful master.

Yes, this song always plunged me into the deepest sadness. The musician declared that he was free to do as he saw fit:

*Na koma libre ehhh*
*Na koma libre eh . . .*
*Liberté eh eh na lingi na sala oyomotem'*
*elingi mama mama . . .*

When the song came to an end I decided I'd better head for home. But as I turned around, my heart skipped a beat: Original Colour was walking into Exotic Music with the Hybrid, arm in arm!

I've never seen a man run so fast. The Hybrid just missed being run over by a car that was parking in front of the record shop. Original Colour took cover with one of her Nigerian girlfriends from the old days, and I walked as far as Les Halles to get a drink at Jip's. My group of pals wasn't there. There was just Paul from the big Congo. As he dozed off in front of his glass of Pelfort, he kept saying:

"Buttocks aren't the only thing in life, there are breasts too . . ."

* * *

We never spoke about that episode at Exotic Music. Even though I sensed Original Colour wanted us to talk about it. From then on, I wasn't allowed to hold our child any more. Original Colour dropped her off with the Cape Verdean childminder on her way to work and picked her up in the evening.

And then, one evening, coming back from Jip's at about half-past midnight, I found the door to our studio open and the lights on. The Hybrid's drums weren't there any more. I could hear my footsteps ringing out as I walked across the floor because Original Colour's things weren't there any more either, and nor were the little one's.

I looked in the Yellow Pages and found the office number for Original Colour's father. I made up my mind to call him in the morning.

But when I got the lawyer from Nancy on the phone he sent me packing, he said that he didn't know who I was and nor did he know the woman or the child I was talking about. He called me a ruffian and a rogue. I remembered the story about that minister Doyen Methuselah. In this lawyer's eyes I was the person who had wrecked the marriage he'd planned between his daughter and the former minister, when it was probably the Hybrid who wrecked his plans at the time.

Yes, I think he must have mistaken me for the Hybrid because as he was hanging up he let rip:

"You pile of shit of an artist! I'll send you back to prison for a second time!"

* * *

Original Colour didn't call me until ten days after she'd

disappeared, to tell me she was in Brazzaville. She was demanding a maintenance allowance and had set the level herself. I talked about it with Paul from the big Congo because I thought Louis-Philippe was too much of a writer to understand the things that go on outside books and the birds in the park trees.

At Jip's, to my great surprise, it was Roger the French-Ivorian who seemed the most receptive. He told me that Original Colour was swindling me, that she was in fact making me pay double the amount as if we'd had twins. And not only that, but he still wanted to know what proof there was that Henriette was my daughter, apart from our toes looking alike? He advised me to pay up all the same because the child wasn't to blame for coming into this world in such chaotic fashion, but I should negotiate the amount down to the last cent. I stared into my glass as I listened to him.

Willy told me he had friends back in the home country, highway bandits who had fought in Angola and Cabinda and who would kill for a piece of cassava or a Marlboro Light, that I shouldn't let the matter drop, that for a fistful of cash those friends of his would be able to rearrange the Hybrid's face, kidnap my daughter and bring her back to me here in Paris.

Yves the just-Ivorian started up again with his stories about the colonial debt.

"This is what it's come to, Buttologist! What am I always saying? Now tell me what you've got out of this relationship! Have you advanced our cause? The colonial debt is still with us because of people like you!"

Pierrot the White said he knew someone who knew someone who knew the lawyer Jacques Vergès, that this lawyer always won his trials, and that he had even defended a Gestapo Chief from Lyon who had organised the deportation of forty-four Jewish children and tortured the Resistance member Jean-Moulin. So all I had to do was consult him . . .

I didn't want to enter into legal wrangling we'd never see the end of. Of course I could go to Brazzaville and settle the matter with machete blows. But that's not my style. I don't like war. I don't like confrontation. Plus the country seemed a long way off to me. I've been gone more than fifteen years now.

And so I chose not to take the path of justice or to make the revenge machete trip. I just pay up without batting an eyelid. I do it for my daughter.

When Original Colour calls me from the home country it's to remind me that in a fortnight it will be the end of the month and I mustn't forget to send "her" allowance. I hang up on her shouting that I'm not a Crédit Agricole cash point, and that it's not her allowance.

But each month I still head for Porte de la Chapelle

to do a Western Union. I queue up with the Malians who are sending all their money back home and who, from what I hear, are building villas over there for their retirement . . .

# III

**E**ach time I sit down to write – at home or in the park nearby – I stare at my typewriter for a long while and think about how I came to buy it, because back when I was always falling out with Original Colour I got to know Louis-Philippe who did book-signings in our neighbourhood, at the Rideau Rouge bookshop. So Roger the French-Ivorian is wrong to think that I started scribbling this diary because of my ex and the Hybrid. Yes they triggered something off in me, and yes psychoanalysts would have tonnes to say on the subject, but I mainly owe everything to meeting Louis-Philippe . . .

I hadn't heard of this writer before. I'm very wary when it comes to contemporary writers, I only read the dead ones, authors who are alive annoy me, they get on my nerves. When you see them on telly they hold forth on whatever they're writing about and they're so smug anyone would think that they had found the philosopher's stone after managing to square the circle or fill the Danaides' jar while standing on their head. Whereas with the dead ones – yes, I know it depends which dead ones – they've written their life's work, they've taken their leave, they lie in peace in graveyards by the sea or at the foot of weeping willows, they let us say what we like about their output because they know that sooner or later we'll have to read them if we don't want to be labelled a dunce by the parents-in-law at the dinner table.

I didn't go to the Rideau Rouge to meet Louis-Philippe, I just happened to be passing by, I was in need of some fresh air because Original Colour was waging a Trojan war against me for the way I'd behaved towards the Hybrid on the day he had worn my Marithé & François Girbaud T-shirt and I'd said it was worth more to me than her ass.

There was a crowd in front of the bookshop. I used to think people were often scared of going into bookshops, what with the risk of coming out with a book they wouldn't read and then being harangued in their sleep by the characters from it who wanted to make them face up to their responsibilities.

So I walked in out of it curiosity. Too bad if I come out with a book I won't read, I thought to myself, and the characters of that book pop up to give me a hard time in my sleep even though we don't know one another.

When Louis-Philippe looked up between signing a couple of books I could tell from his smile that he was happy to see me there, probably because writers are all the same, I'll never understand them, they're good at making the people who are about to become their readers believe they even know the date of their birthday.

He winked at me, as if to say he'd clocked me, that I mustn't get away. So I wandered around between the piles of books. There were girls eyeing him voraciously, and he was flashing his seductive smile. I was taking a good look at the backsides of these female readers, and trying to figure out if any of them had come for something more than getting their book signed. Louis-Philippe had a joke for each of them, he took his time choosing the words he scribbled on the first page of the book.

We could hear his deep voice:

"Should I be dedicating this to your husband as well?"

"Oh, I'm not married!" simpered the single woman.

The bookshop owner noticed that my gaze was on the rear assets of the reader standing in front of Louis-Phillippe. She looked embarrassed and, to help her out of an awkward moment, I grabbed Louis-Philippe's book, *Dream of A Childhood Photo*, and went over to the till. She wanted to explain what the book was about, but I wasn't really paying attention. She also caught me soaking up the B-side of a very fidgety brunette now standing opposite the writer. I was trying to work out if her butt was like Original Colour's or if it just had a manual gearbox. Boy, was that brunette dragging out the conversation. No one else existed in her eyes. Given the way Louis-Philippe was looking at her, I thought: my god, this story is going to end up in the sack in a hotel on Rue des Petites Écuries.

To kill time I re-read the title of Louis-Philippe's book that I was holding. It was warm and tender: *Dream of A Childhood Photo* . . .

\* \* \*

Half an hour later the brunette was still narrating how her ninety-eight-year-old uncle had been to Haiti, how he had adopted a young Haitian who now works for the Post Office in Nantes, how he'd also helped several Haitians flee Papa Doc's regime, and then Baby Doc's, how he'd been initiated by the great voodoo practitioners, how he owned naïve paintings by some Pétionville artists, how his favourite book was *Country Without A Hat* by Dany Laferrière because it captures the spirit of Haiti, it's chock-a-block with proverbs, and there are people in the street who are in fact zombies and all that kind of thing. The elderly uncle in question had met the author of *Country Without A Hat* in person, a brilliant, witty man who never knew whether he should be living in Miami or Montreal. Louis-Philippe didn't want the brunette to think that he was in the least bit bothered by her flaunting the merits of another Haitian author, when he was there to sign his own books.

He forced a smile and said:

"Dany Laferrière is a great friend! I would urge you to read another of his books: *How To Make Love To A Negro Without Getting Tired*..."

A redhead cut short their conversation. She glared with blood red eyes at the brunette who realised she'd better scat and fast. The brunette left the bookshop muttering to herself, with one book by Dany Laferrière but none by Louis-Philippe.

The redhead had a more direct approach. She grabbed a stool, sat bang opposite the author and proceeded to tell him that she took some of his books to bed with her, especially *God's Pencil Has No Eraser*. She even felt as if he was writing them for her, that she was one of his characters.

"I want a proper dedication, none of that 'With best wishes from the author' nonsense! I want a dedication intended for me and me alone. This is a book I'll read every night before going to sleep, even if there's a guy lying next to me . . ."

Louis-Philippe looked up at the ceiling and then wrote something. He held out the book to the redhead who immediately read the dedication. She blushed, kissed the author on the cheek and left the Rideau Rouge waving at him in a knowing kind of a way.

I was staring at her B-side and thinking to myself: "That one's a dormant volcano!"

* * *

After taking his leave of the bookshop owner, Louis-Philippe made his way over to me. I had his book tucked under my arm. He called me "old buddy".

When I told him that I lived in the area he nearly exploded:

"That means we're neighbours! I don't live far. We must swap phone numbers. Drop by whenever you want, you've got to try my Barbancourt rum from back home!"

We left the bookshop, walked up Rue Riquet and grabbed a table at the Roi du Café. I had my back to Rue Marx Dormoy, so I could see in his eyes the marks he was giving the backside of each girl as she crossed the road. This was all we talked about, the different kinds of B-sides. And he was having a good laugh with it.

That evening I arrived back home feeling light-hearted and it didn't bother me that Mr Hippocratic was lying in wait. the Hybrid had already left for the night, I wasn't interested in finding out why. I started reading even though Original Colour complained that the light would wake the little one. I was far away, I wasn't in that studio any more. Everything around me stopped existing. I was picturing Louis-Philippe's island, Haiti. I was the character from the capital of Port-au-Prince which he had re-named Port-of-Filth. He had painted the portrait of Pointe-Noire, where I come from. The people looked like me. I underlined everything. I was in a state of wonder before the poetry of his language.

I called Louis-Philippe the next day. I went over to his place, and I got to drink Barbancourt for the first time. I admired his bookshelves, I leafed through each of his books that had been published. He teased me a bit about my outfit.

"Do the Congolese always dress like that?"

The following day after I went to buy a typewriter from Porte de Vincennes because I don't like computers, and because I wanted to be like a real writer who rips up pages, crosses things out, and has to interrupt his creative flow in order to change the typewriter ribbon . . .

* * *

When Original Colour nagged me for spending too much time writing, hanging out at Jip's and only working part-time at the printing works, I'd just get up and take my typewriter for a walk in the park. I would sit on a bench under a street lamp along with the tramps who were knocking back bottles of red, and I'd keep on writing.

I think I must have been hitting the keys too hard because even the tramps were giving me funny looks, as if they thought I was losing the plot and would soon be joining them. I kept on writing, I was writing more and more. When I saw a bird moving in a branch, I would write it down. When it flew off to another tree, I wrote that down too because Louis-Philippe who knew a thing or two about inspiration had told me that writers noted everything down and then went through their notes so they only kept the stuff that really mattered. Thanks to him I was now reading like a bookworm, I wasn't just reading dead authors, I was reading living ones too, I really wanted to become a writer in the vein of Georges Simenon whose Maigret adventures had been all the way round the world. But then I realised that I could only write about what I'd experienced, about what there was around me, and that it would have to be every bit as chaotic . . .

f I had several encounters only a month after Original Colour left, it was because I felt very angry and I wanted to get my own back. I'm not the kind of person who thinks that revenge is a dish best eaten cold. I don't like all that biblical patter about how you've got to turn the other cheek when someone slaps you. I grab the bull by the horns.

So off I went hunting in our community's nightclubs and at the concerts of Koffi Olomide and Papa Wemba. But I came home empty-handed and started to feel despondent, it was as if I had lost my charm and I wondered about the sand slipping through my fingers. I risked becoming a man of the past. There were good-for-nothings out there who knotted their ties better than me, and they were more forward too. I started believing my misfortune was written on my forehead where Original Colour had put a curse on me.

And then someone rose to the bait one evening at the Keur Samba nightclub, in the 8th arrondissement. That's where I ran into Rose. She had arrived from the Congo a month earlier, and there was no mistaking it when you saw her on the dance floor, she looked like someone who, instead of being descended from the apes like everyone else, was heading back that way for good. She hopped about, opened her arms and legs wide before landing down on the ground. At the end she was sweating so much I was turned off by the sweat stains on her white blouse. There were a few compatriots chasing after her, and she was playing hard to get, she'd lead them into a corner before coming back to dance opposite me. It was all a show, I'd clicked that she was available and that I was the one she was enticing with this dance of the spear-wielding caveman hunting the mammoth.

What have I got to lose, eh, I thought to myself, by indulging in a bit of pleasure this evening? I'm being provoked, so I have to defend myself, and attack is the best line of defence.

I stood up and tried to dance a few centimetres away from her, imitating her prehistoric movements. I held out my hand, she turned her back to me: it was all about proving she wasn't an easy catch.

I sat back down again, what else could I do, I'd rather have died than carry on following her jerky moves and strops.

My withdrawal strategy paid off, Rose came over to me:

"Is that how they try to pick you up in Paris? The girl gets a bit stroppy and the man goes to sit back down again without putting up a fight? Come on, come and dance the tchakoulibonda with me!"

She could see that I wasn't familiar with that particular dance. You had to shake your shoulders, grab your partner by the waist and simulate a violent penetration from the B-side. Apparently, it was all the rage back in the home country. I've never felt so ridiculous in my life. The entire nightclub was looking at me and I thought I could hear people creasing up with laughter.

Towards two in the morning I suggested to Rose that we go and drink a last glass back at my place.

"Cut the patter, you want do the business, I can tell! I'm not a little girl any more, I've got a sixteen-year-old kid back home!"

I thought the game was up, but she went to fetch her bag which her cousin was looking after. I heard her say to him:

"I won't be coming home this evening, but don't worry, the guy I'm leaving with is a big brother. He's a softie, he's not going to cause me any trouble."

We caught a taxi not far from Fouquet's. I didn't say anything as we were crossing the city, and nor did she. I was picturing Original Colour again, and wondering what she was up to right then back in the home country with the Hybrid.

The taxi dropped us off in front of the Arab on the corner's, which was closed at that hour.

I was praying that Mr Hippocratic wouldn't wake up as I opened the door to my studio.

Rose just stood there on the threshold.

"Aren't you going to turn on the light?"

"We don't need it," I answered, "come in."

"We don't know each other well, and I'm not happy being in the dark like this with a stranger, I've heard lots of weird stories . . ."

She flicked the switch and the light dazzled us. I got a good look at her close-up and wondered if this was the same woman as before. At Keur Samba she'd looked so young, her skin as soft as a suckling babe's. And in the violet light of the disco club her wraparound skirt showed off her B-side nicely. What I hadn't noticed was that her skin had been put through some kind of chemical peel, and her hair and nails were fake.

"Turn the light off, please," I said.

"How are you going to know I'm beautiful if there isn't any light?"

So we left the light on. She got undressed quickly. I didn't want my eyes to spend too long on her breasts, which were covered in stretchmarks like the slashes you find on the Téké faces back home.

I lay down on the bed but leaving a big gap between her and me, and I just stared at the ceiling.

"When are we starting? Anyone would think you weren't hot for me any more . . . Come here!"

I started to touch her.

"No, no, no, don't stroke me, I'm not a White girl! That doesn't arouse me, it just makes me giggle and then it gets annoying . . ."

When she said that, my thing down there didn't want to rise any more, it contracted into my testicles and I couldn't imagine what extraordinary event might bring it back out of its storeroom.

Rose asked me if there was a problem.

"No, everything's fine, everything's fine . . ."

"So what are we waiting for?"

"Let's sleep, we'll do it tomorrow, it's better that way."

"What? There won't be a tomorrow with me! Not on my life! Who do you take me for? You aroused me at Keur Samba and now you want to leave me in this state? Why did you bring me back to your place if you can't go through with it? Do you know how many people wanted to do it with me today, eh, people I sent packing because I wanted it to be with you?"

"Listen, I'm not feeling on form, and I'm not going to force things!"

"So what does it take? When a normal man sees a naked woman it starts up right away. Are you a man or not? So let me touch your thing down there, you'll soon get in the mood, you'll see . . ."

"No!"

"Are you saying NO to me???"

She leapt out of bed like a wounded tigress. She put her clothes back on as quickly as she'd taken them off.

"Idiot! Jerk! I thought time-wasters like you only existed back home, not here in Paris. You were well dressed with a suit and tie but you can't even give a girl a good poking. What's the point of your thing down there? Just for pissing, is it? Stupid bastard! Give me my taxi fare or I'll smash everything in here and scream out in the hallway!"

I stood up to take a note out of my jacket pocket. I held it out to her, she tore it off me while spitting in my face.

"That's so you'll remember me! I'm Rose, and I'll say it again, you're a stupid bastard, I don't know what kind of woman goes out with a guy like you!"

She slammed the door. Luckily, Mr Hippocratic didn't bang on the wall . . .

* * *

And I also remember the day when, together with Vladimir the Cameroonian who smokes the longest cigars in France and Navarre, the two of us played at being princes at Atlantis, a club in the 13th arrondissement on the Quai d'Austerlitz. It's Vladimir the Cameroonian's stronghold, he gets the red-carpet treatment there, and he's even allowed to smoke his cigars inside. So I could make out I owned the place too. Seeing as Vladimir never does things by halves, we hired a Mercedes and a BMW that evening.

Once we'd been seated in the VIP corner, Vladimir brought over a girl who was tall and skinny as a broom handle and he whispered in my ear:

"This one's a real daddy's girl, I want you to whip her

ass tonight! Drink some gin and tonic, you're going to be up 'til dawn and, believe me, this girl won't forget it . . ."

Gwendoline was the daughter of a Gabonese minister. As soon as we'd been introduced she started talking about her daddy's second homes, and about her own travels around the world. There wasn't a corner on earth she hadn't set foot in, she told me.

"When I'm at my father's house I don't touch a thing, not even a plate, we have servants, I have a driver, the hairdresser comes specially to our house with her six assistants."

And so Vladimir left me in the claws of this daddy's girl. She made me want to sneeze with her perfume that stank of the Mananas we use on corpses back home. I could spot my friend winking at me from a long way off, between the swirls of his cigar smoke. But there was no stopping Gwendoline. I let her carry on with the stocktaking of her paternal inheritance. I even got to find out what kind of plates and forks they had at home. Then she fell quiet because she could see I wasn't impressed.

"You're not very chatty, are you? You haven't told me your name . . ."

"Buttologist."

"I beg your pardon?"

"My friends call me Buttologist . . ."

She nearly swallowed an ice cube as big as a ping-pong ball.

"Are you joking or what? Right, well, I'd better call you what everyone else does! Vladimir told me you're not just anybody. I understand that Mercedes Kompressor convertible in front of the night club is yours?"

I didn't tell her we'd rented the car. I pretended to be the owner. I jangled the keys while whistling *Another Day in Paradise* by Phil Collins. I was smoking a Cohiba cigar and blowing smoke rings above my head.

She asked me what my line of work was.

"Businessman . . ."

"Really? What kind of business?"

"I sell diamonds to jewellers on the Place Vendôme. In a nutshell, I sell eternity because diamonds are forever . . ."

"My mother adores diamonds!"

I had scored a point. During the zouk love numbers, she clung to me like a leech. I'd never had anybody hit on me this hard. By the end I'd had enough, and I wanted to hover around two or three other girls who were tall as wading birds and kept on giving me lighthouse signals from across the dance floor. Nothing doing, Gwendoline had found her diamond dealer and she wasn't going to let him out of her clutches.

"Diamonds! And do you sell gold as well?"

"Now and then. But frankly, gold is for small-timers. It's not like diamonds, which are forever. And another thing, even if people say everything that glitters is not gold, they still go for the glitter. But diamonds don't glitter, they diffuse light, and that's why they're the preserve of connoisseurs . . ."

"Aren't you the smooth talker? I'm not buying a diamond now! But since you're in the trade, perhaps you could finally explain something to me because I've never understood this business of twenty-four carats which everyone talks about but no one . . ."

"We're here to have a good time . . . If things carry on like this, I'll sell you a diamond and this evening could end up being very expensive for you!"

I wanted to catch my breath, but there she was behind me, staring at me as if I were a god. She shot envious looks at the Congolese women who recognised me. And I chose to pour oil on the flames. I zoned in on the ladies I knew, and threw myself into long conversations with them to prove I had my harem about me. Behaving jealously, as if we went back many a full moon together, Gwendoline came over to separate me from my little crowd. Even when we were dancing with our arms wrapped round each other, I was still treated to the fast-track biography of "The Minister" and his unstoppable ascent to power.

She wouldn't let it drop:

"My father? He's a very important lawyer, the most important lawyer in Africa! He is respected by the Whites! At the time when he did his studies, you could count the Blacks in French universities on the fingers of one hand. Of course there were Blacks in France, but they were road-sweepers, packers, gardeners, dockers in Marseille or Le Havre, factory workers for Simca, Peugeot, Citroën and Renault . . ."

I nodded, which only encouraged her.

"My father? You've got to meet him to understand what a truly exceptional man he is! He paid for my studies in this country's elite establishments. I couldn't love a man more than him! He is everything to me. He knew Pompidou, he knew the black members of the National Assembly at the time, your Senghors, your Boignys and others who would go on to become president in their own countries. My father was so brilliant that high office was thrust upon him straight away, and he's been in government for more than twenty-five years now. He is the only minister the president can't fire because he's responsible for the country's politically sensitive files. And if he opens those files, even the French government would come toppling down in less than five minutes!"

What she didn't realise was that like most Africans who followed the continent's current affairs a bit, I knew that Mr Bigshot Lawyer had been named Minister of Justice in order to carry out a specific mission: changing the country's constitution every time the dictator president asked him to. He wrote the Constitution of his country in a single session because their president was obsessed with overtaking the French Constitution of the Fifth Republic. According to this Head of State, de Gaulle, who was applauded by everybody in Africa, had messed up his Constitution, and the French had taken advantage of this by showing him a lack of respect at the end of the sixties. Mr Bigshot Lawer had the original idea of giving all the powers to the President of the Republic. And so the President is at the same time Prime Minister, Cabinet Minister, Minister of Defence, Minister of the Interior, Finance Minister and above all Minister of Oil and Hydrocarbons.

While Gwendoline was bragging about daddy's villas and fleet of cars, I was listening to her with one ear, and telling myself that the hour would strike when I'd make her be quiet and we'd finally get down to serious business. She would no longer be the minister's daughter, with her taste for fancy cars and travels. She would be a naked woman in front of a naked man, and there, all human beings have the same weapons . . .

Looking back on it, I think what matters is that I managed to get Gwendoline into the car and that we slept on the fifth floor of the Novotel in Porte de Bagnolet, in a suite. I gave the excuse of having left my card in the car, so she was the one who guaranteed the room.

"Tomorrow, after lunch, I'll get the money out at a cash point," I promised her.

The minister's daughter kept disappearing off into the bathrooms, drinking champagne and letting out idiotic peals of laughter in front of a television programme about the laborious mating rituals of the Zimbabwean rhinoceros.

She started up again with her question about the
twenty-four carats. I explained to her that a carat was
the amount of gold contained in an alloy and that
amount was expressed as a twenty-fourth of the total
weight. She stared at me, wide-eyed. But I knew we'd
never see each other again. Because I didn't like her
derrière that only wiggled on one side. And because the
way she went on about her old man would get on my
nerves . . .

At five in the morning, while she was sound asleep, I
tiptoed out of the hotel. All she's got to do is call her father,
I reasoned, and he can settle the bill from Libreville . . .

I still go and visit Louis-Philippe because it makes a change from my pals at Jip's. Talking of which, I must remember to give him back his copy of *The Dirty Havana Trilogy*, I've had it for a while now. He's a real writer, and it's not just the regulars at the Rideau Rouge who enjoy what he writes. I've got him to read a good chunk of what I've written so far. He's told me I'm not there yet, that I've got to learn how to structure my ideas instead of writing when driven by anger or bitterness.

"We don't write to take our revenge, you have to master your anger and contain it so that your prose flows naturally. Deep down, I'm sure you really loved Original Colour, and you still do love her, don't you?"

There was nothing I could say. I looked at him for a moment, this man who was so far away from his island, who had taken leave of his nearest and dearest years ago. I wondered why Haitians are either brilliant writers or taxi drivers for life in New York and Miami. And when they're writers they are in exile. Do writers always have to live in another country, and preferably be forced to live there so that they've got things to write about and other people can analyse the influence of exile on their writing? Why doesn't Louis-Philippe live in New York or Miami?

Sometimes I sing *Armstrong* to him, in which a famous singer from Toulouse, Claude Nougaro, has almost the same trouble as me with inspiration, except it's about skin colour for him:

> *Armstrong, I am no black man*
> *I am white of skin*
> *When I want to sing on hope*
> *My luck is not in*
> *Yes, I can see the birds and the sky*
> *But nothing, nothing glimmers on high*
> *I am white of skin*

Louis-Philippe tells me that without homesickness nothing comes out, even if you can see the restless birds in the branches. Now it just so happens that I am also far from my country, and I feel like I'm in exile, so am I going to spend my life crying about this? These Haitian writers are like hunted birds. They've had more than thirty-two coups d'état back home and not a country in the world has equalled this record yet. With each coup d'état, flocks of writers have emigrated. They left everything behind, setting out with nothing apart from their manuscripts and their driving licence. I wish I'd been born Haitian so I could be a writer in exile who understands the song of the migrating bird, but I don't have any manuscripts, or a driving licence to become, in the worst-case scenario, a taxi driver in the streets of Paris . . .

* * *

When Louis-Philippe talks about his country, his eyes go moist with emotion. I've got received ideas, clichés in black and white, as well as colour snapshots too. Life there has its ups and downs. When he tells me about how their country was the first black Republic, I applaud, I feel proud as a Toussaint Louverture painted by Edouard Duval-Carrié, the most rated Haitian artist in Miami. But I stop clapping when Louis-Philippe talks to me about the Tonton Macoutes and company. Ouch, I screech, ouch, papa Duvalier and son? Uncle Aristide not at all Catholic?

I filled Louis-Philippe in on how, over in the Congo, we know a few tunes from his native country, we grew up with his music. You could hear the voice of their musician Coupé singing "Away with you" in all our bars. And when we heard "Away with you", it meant it was dawn and the bar was about to close. But there were always those last remaining gentlemen who deliberately ignored Coupé Cloué even though he told them several times: "Away with you! Away with you! Away with you!" Coupé Cloué is a sort of Haitian Manu Dibango, the same shaved head, the same smile that reaches all the way to his ears.

I also listened to the rhythms of their group Skah
Shah de New York with Jean Elie Telfort's voice,
because I'm an open-minded kind of guy after all who
is thoughtful about the ways of the world. I enjoyed
the song *Camionnette* by Claudette et Ti Pierre, and
whenever I heard that summer hit it meant there was
a burial or a party to mark the end of the mourning
period in our neighbourhood, and sometimes even
a wedding because we're like that back home, in life
and death we dance to the same rhythm for funerals,
weddings, divorces and for the other joys and trials of
everyday life. There is joy in pain, that's the way it is in
my small country . . .

* * *

I won't easily forget how guilty I felt for not knowing how
to dance the Haitian kompa properly. Not that there was
anything fancy about this dance, all you had to do was
grab your partner by the hips and make a compass with
her, the way we used to in geometry at elementary school,
that was it. Easy to say but difficult out there on the dance
floor. And I admitted to Louis-Philippe that I'd had to
make my excuses to the only Haitian lady in our district of
Trois-Cents. This woman was stunned to see that a negro
from the Congo didn't know how to dance the kompa,
even though everybody knows that all black music comes
from Africa and there's no point in teaching Africans how
to dance because it comes naturally as soon as the music

starts up. And this Haitian lady was called Mirabelle. She said she was going to teach me the basics. And I said great, at last I'm going to be able to dance the kompa.

Mirabelle had an enormous and very firm B-side, it was easy to grab hold of and let yourself be carried like a baby kangaroo stuffed inside its mother's pocket.

"Hold on tight, little one," she said to me, "or you'll fall off when things heat up. Don't be shy and don't hold back. If you feel something rising up between your legs, don't be ashamed, it's only natural, it means you're starting to master the kompa."

So I squeezed her tight in order to rub myself up against her as best I could. But I was dancing the Congolese rumba and that annoyed her.

She shouted:

"The Congolese rumba isn't the only thing in life, there's the kompa too."

And I answered:

"No one can learn a dance in one day . . ."

"Dance this kompa for me instead of talking! Squeeze me hard in the upright position, make like you're rising up and sinking down while lightly brushing against my chest. But watch it, I don't want you crushing my breasts!"

And then she said I had to go a bit faster than that, that I had to wrap my arms around her, and glue my face to hers. I applied myself: I was sweating, she was sweating, we were spinning, we were colliding with the other dancers, we were heading for the wall, then for a dark corner where she took the opportunity to stuff her hand between my legs and declare with a big smile:

"I see that now you have mastered the kompa! I didn't know you could learn so quickly! There's something growing hard between your legs . . ."

At least I saved face that day. But I still can't dance the kompa properly because I always tread on the toes of my partners – especially Haitians from Pétionville . . .

\* \* \*

Like me, Louis-Philippe has got a moustache. He wears glasses for being short-sighted, I don't, which is only to be expected because he's read more books than Roger the French-Ivorian, especially the Latin American writers. And he also maintains that a writer should wear reading glasses so people can tell he's really working, that it's all he does, that he sweats, because people won't believe you're a writer if you haven't got reading glasses. So it's hardly surprising if I wear clear glasses now, it makes it easier for people to imagine I'm short-sighted.

The day Louis-Philippe saw me with these glasses, he chuckled:

"It's true I said in jest that you should wear glasses to fit with the image the general public has of a writer, but you didn't have to go and buy the most expensive pair on Rue du Faubourg Saint-Honoré!"

When I turn up at his place, he can't wait to show me the

most recent naïve Haitian paintings he's brought back from his island. And we talk about everything. I say bad things about Mr Hippocratic. And explain how I'd like to move out of the building that has ruined my life.

Louis-Philippe thinks that, now Original Colour is no longer there, I should try talking to Mr Hippocratic from time to time.

"Mr Hippocratic is desperate, he's the kind of person who only wants to hold your hand, but he doesn't know how to go about it, especially with you. Try to reassure him, to make a friend you can talk to. Remember he's a brother in colour, even if he doesn't know it . . ."

**M**y pals from Jip's know how prudent I am when it comes to money. I only spend what I've got and I don't covet other people's possessions. I don't want to owe anything to anyone. I refuse to be tempted by our consumer society. So I don't like loans, whether we're talking simple or compound repayments or by instalment, I don't like credit cards with payments either deferred or not, I don't like overdrafts that pretend they only cost you cents when the more cents stacked up by the banker the more the debt piles up. Cents are a bit like the yeast that makes the dough rise. Behind these loans, behind these cards and these overdrafts there are always shady schemes even if the banker has the friendliest smile in the world and suggests you pop over to the café right opposite his bank's cashpoint. When a professional invites you to join him for a coffee like that, it's so he can have you by the short and afro-curlies. It's not expensive, the café opposite a financial institution, but you're still the one who pays for it in the end. The thing about yeast is that you can't see when it makes the dough rise, you wake up one morning and it's already spilling over the edges. They add on interest for this and that to the coffee you drank on a day you can't even remember any more, a coffee that wasn't even black and that was served up in something as small as a Coca-Cola bottle-top . . .

Deferred repayments? Overdrafts? I know what's inside those scalding hot cooking pots and how it all turns out. The men and women who end up paying off the whole debt are few and far between. Or why would the banks push us into placing the rope around our necks instead of them staking all that money on the stock exchange and leaving us alone in our poverty?

I've rumbled their business model: nowadays, poverty has become the best investment for a financial institution, there's no point in buying apartments and putting tenants inside any more, you've got to invest in poverty. Soon you'll be able to buy shares in it on the Paris Stock Exchange, and the shareholders, including the small investors, will make a killing . . .

I pay my taxes on time because I don't want the bailiffs turning up at my door with a sinister-looking locksmith. There's nothing worse than an ill-timed visit from these people with their long faces who proceed to itemise your hi-fi, your old typewriter bought from a second-hand shop in Porte de Vincennes, your electric toothbrush and your Italian cafetière.

Did I say bailiffs? Their grey suits get up my nose, I'm sure they always wear the same one. Their thick glasses try my patience, I get the feeling they can stare right into my body, and that they can part my bones to see if I'm hiding a secret stash of money between my growth plates. As for the injunction letters, they stop you from sleeping at night because you can never understand them even if you read them a hundred times with the latest Code of Civil Procedure right in front of you. There's always a last minute article or a subtle qualification, the upshot of which is to make you pay the call-out fee for the sinister-looking locksmith as well as the administrative costs of the bailiff in the grey suit that gets up your nose . . .

In short, I am a man whose generosity knows no limits. Original Colour didn't understand this. I give money to the beggars who sit in front of the mosque at Château Rouge. Why them? Well, because I prefer them to the beggars who wear me out in the métro because you have to wonder if they aren't laying it on a bit thick. The beggars in the métro are aggressive, they accuse you of being responsible for their misfortune and they think you owe them something. Some of them even go right ahead and insult you.

I came across one on Line 4. He was as old as the prophets in the Old Testament who used to live for longer than we do. It was as if he'd been following me for several stops. Was it because I was well dressed or because I looked like I was a pushover? Maybe. Maybe not. In any case I slipped him a few coins because he told me he hadn't eaten for four days and four and a half nights. I was happy to have done a good deed. I felt light-hearted and I held it against the other passengers for not smiling at him because a smile is the key to life after all, as our Arab on the corner likes to point out.

When the métro stopped at Etienne Marcel, the guy waved at me as he got off. He didn't realise I was getting out at the same stop. I watched him rush into the nearest Arab on the corner's and grab a bottle of red wine, which he started necking before my eyes. What a swindle, I thought, this guy hasn't put my cash to good use. I won't allow myself to be hoodwinked ever again by beggars in the métro.

So that's why I prefer the beggars at the mosque in Château Rouge. They won't get blind drunk like that. The eye watching Cain will prevent them. They're not aggressive, they don't insult anybody, they don't ask, they wait to be given something. And when you give, there is only the beggar and Allah witnessing this heartfelt act . . .

* * *

I'm not a fearful person, I don't lack courage or open-spiritedness. It's a question of strategy: a living coward is worth more than a dead hero. This was a very sensible piece of advice given to me by my deceased uncle who had deserted the army camp during the Biafran War because he wanted to defend his humble being and die a slow death rather than for ideas that'll be obsolete in a few years as Georges Brassens, the singer with the moustache, puts it. I've realised that desertion runs in my family because I too fled military service in my country of origin. Weapons and all that, it's not my thing. In fact, when I spot a man in uniform – even the security guards at a shopping mall or for the cash machine of a local bank – I cross over to the other side, I pick up the pace and I don't look back. I imagine World War Three is at hand, that troops are moving towards Porte de la Chapelle, that the famous Senegalese soldiers will be called to the rescue as they were in the old days. That's why I hate war films, however brilliant the director. The last one I saw was *Saving Private Ryan*. Yes, it was a bit different from *The Longest Day* which was in black and white, but it was still a war film, there were uniforms, weapons and all that, explosives, detonations and human flesh galore and all tightly plotted, but in a proper war there's no plot, there's no close-ups, there's no wide-angle shots, there's no classic dialogue, people shoot themselves and the dead get counted so the historians from the Sorbonne and future generations won't bicker about the exact number of victims.

One of my childhood friends who advised me to do my military service over in Angola – and even to get myself recruited as a soldier – claimed that being in the military was a cushy number because during wars the soldier has a better chance of survival than a civilian who, on top of everything else, will die without honours. But I love peace, I'd far rather die a civilian and be buried in a communal grave. Someone once recommended if you wish for peace, prepare for war. I don't agree with him. For me the person who wishes for peace must prepare for peace, end of story, the word war is surplus to requirements. And on that subject I have a photo of Martin Luther King somewhere in my suitcases. And in that photo, the black preacher is standing in front of a picture of Gandhi . . .

But back in the home country they were making us go to Angola to fight the war – they tried to cover up this up by saying we were going there to do our military service, and that we needed to be ready in case our neighbours the Zairians, who are a lot more numerous than us, attacked us to steal our oil, our timber and even our Atlantic Ocean.

It was at the time when we had to help the Angolans who were fighting against their rebel Jonas Savimbi and his men hidden in the maquis. So our government sent our young men to Luanda in their masses. We saw this as a punishment since the children of prominent citizens and other powerful figures in the regime didn't have to go, not them. And Jonas Savimbi's rebels hadn't done anything to me to make me hunt them in the bush where they survived by hunting, gathering and fishing. Better still, I admired Jonas Savimbi's big beard, his big nose and his green mamba eyes. I was happy when he routed the Angolan armed forces, and I crossed my fingers for him to win the war. Why go and fight against someone you like?

If us plebs were in a hurry to go to Angola it was in the hope of clearing off to Europe from our neighbouring country, which was a den of traffickers working hand in glove with the airlines. All you had to do was raise the tidy sum of three hundred thousand CFA francs, and you could fly off to Europe. I managed to get the hell out for good from Luanda.

I first arrived in Portugal before washing up in Belgium, and then in France with the ID of a long dead compatriot whose brothers had sold his residency card to Angolan traffickers. I go by the surname and first name of this disappeared person, so you'll understand if I haven't revealed my real name up until this point, still less the name of the street where my little studio in the 18th arrondissement is located. Obviously, the day I kick the bucket my little brother who lives in the home country will rush to sell my papers to the Angolans who will, in turn, sell them on to some idiot keen to make the journey to Europe.

But look, I'm in good shape and good health, and my wake isn't set for tomorrow . . .

* * *

I don't enjoy recalling those times of sacrifice, the work I did well in spite of myself before going to Angola. I would get up in the morning and wait for a truck in front of a bus shelter opposite Studio-Photo Vicky, on Independence Avenue. I would climb up onto the truck together with some other guys. The truck would purr its way along the Avenue, stopping every two hundred metres to pick up more packers. By the time we reached the town centre, day would be slowly breaking. We could hear the waves roaring. The sea was just metres away. The fish sellers in the Grand Market would be parking their old bangers at the entrance to the port and waiting, anxiously, for the return of the Beninese who had the monopoly on fishing the Côte Sauvage. The natives thought it was a humiliating job. That was the sea for you. Fights breaking out between fish sellers, arguments that ended in fisticuffs in the middle of the ocean ...

This was where I worked, having failed my baccalauréat in Letters and Philosophy and my father having concluded that school wasn't for me, that in any case it was a factory for turning out the unemployed along with people who wanted to become President of the Republic when in our country if you wanted to become President all you had to learn was how to execute a coup d'état and put your tribe in charge.

The truck would tip us out on the roadside like

sardines, and we would walk up to a barrier where men in uniform would check our identity, confiscate our bags, and only then let us through in single file. And so the hard day's work began, with the unloading of containers watched over by foremen. We were endlessly being accused of stealing objects from abroad in order to sell them on in Trois-Cents. At the slightest theft, the guilty person would be marched to the main customs office where he was stripped before being whipped with barbed wire and then a final settlement would be drawn up making him a debtor for life. With so many objects from all over the world the temptation to steal was there, no doubt about it. But it was the customs officers who indulged in this trafficking, we were just scapegoats. We the subordinates, we the less-than-nothings could only covet those marvels from a distance . . .

At one o'clock in the afternoon we were finally allowed to stop for a bite to eat. But even during our break, the foremen stuck to us like leeches. On each table they put a monster of a guard with a weightlifter's physique, who chewed big chunks of cassava, had a swivelling eye and was listening out for the slightest whisper. We didn't leave the port until evening, after interminable searches during which each worker was made to wear his birthday suit and put his hands in the air in a hut we nicknamed the "Screening House". When we stepped outside, we felt as if we'd passed a tax inspection with flying colours.

At night, you had to sleep to be in good shape again for the next day . . .

*  *  *

My father would often impress on me that nothing was easy in a man's life. Earning my living at the port had the advantage of toughening me up, and of making me think before spending. And he cited the example of my uncle Jean-Pierre Matété who had spent years humping goods at the Pointe-Noire railway station. That was how he had succeeded in life. He had built a permanent house, owned a water pump, and had electricity. And to complete his happiness, he had gone to find the woman of his life back in the village because, as he reminded us, "women from the town marry the wallet".

My father had ideas about success that I no longer shared as the years went by. For him, the ideal was to have a job, any job. You had to put money aside for a few years, and then build a permanent house before returning to your birth village to marry a submissive virgin and a good housewife. The money you had saved would be used for the dowry, of course. And indeed this was how he had married my mother. He had told me this story to buck me up, to give me courage for my job at the port . . .

I can see this man, my father, now. Stocky, kindly looking, he had been lucky enough to reach the second year of elementary school, which meant he could express himself in French at a level envied by many of his friends. His work as a houseboy for the Europeans in the town centre was a sort of revenge, an opportunity to prove to the old people in the neighbourhood that he had succeeded in life. What's more, he used to label all those old folks as "Australopithecus" because in his view they had closed minds, with no culture or vision about the big problems in our world. He had often thought that serving, obeying, being in the company of, and listening behind the doors of the Whites had raised him to the pinnacle of western civilisation whereby he had an opinion on everything and nothing. As long as the Whites had said something, then it had to be true, and it was impossible to present him with evidence to the contrary, particularly if that evidence came from a negro.

He would lose his temper:

"The White man is not stupid! Believe me, I am in their company every working day."

And so, unassailable, he would launch into his explanations:

"There are Whites of every colour! Some have strange marks on their faces, some have very white hair even though they are still young, some have skin as white as palm wine, some have a skin that makes you wonder if they even deserve to be Whites, some even turn blue instead of going red when they are angry or embarrassed! The Whites, they come in every colour, take it from me! I'd even go so far as to say that Whites aren't white the way people think they are!"

He told whoever wanted to hear it that he could have married a White woman, a "real" one who would have taken him to live in France, in Bordeaux. Why Bordeaux and not another French town? Because of the wine. To this day he believes that the town owes its name to the wine and that all the wines on earth, as long as they're red, are automatically bordeaux wines that come from Bordeaux. He still doesn't know that there are white bordeaux wines. And another thing, when he went inside one of the refreshment stalls in Trois-Cents and wanted to have a drink, a "long" or a "short" red from the Congolese Wine Society, he would call out to the bar owner: "A glass of bordeaux!"

At the time, he used to drink like a sponge. He stopped drinking the year I left for Angola, following a heart scare that nearly cost him his life. When he got drunk back then and started rowing with my mother, I'd hear him saying over and over again:

"If I'd known, I would have married a White woman from Bordeaux! At least with her I'd be able to drink my bordeaux without people giving me grief . . ."

But he was destined to spend his life with our mother. He had found a stall for her at the Grand Market, and she sold groundnuts, salt fish and palm oil. I am the first fruit of this marriage arranged by the notables from our village of Louboulou. My brother was born five years later. They all live back in the country, in Pointe-Noire.

I haven't set eyes on any of them for over fifteen years, but I can still remember my mother's last words to me, as she wept:

"Go to France, work and send me a little money so that I can rent a big stall at the Tié-Tié Market. And then, give me a grandson or a granddaughter before I leave this earth for ever . . ."

**S**eeing as I've got the time now, when I'm not writing or having my drink at Jip's I like to lose myself in the Marché Dejean, at Château Rouge, and to remember it was here that Original Colour and her friend Rachel used to sell salt fish on the sly. I spot some characters from the home country. Plenty arrive on foot from the Gare du Nord. In summer the sun seems to roast them, poor things, but it takes more than that to change their habits. They walk, they like to take their time getting there. They're unlikely to buy anything at the market but, like me, they will feel as if they're back in the home country, listening to our rural languages, exchanging banter about life in France, about dictators sucking the continent dry and inciting different ethnic groups to tear each other's guts out before the cameras of the international community.

My Gare du Nord compatriots step off the trains from the banlieues, survey the Boulevard Magenta, peer through the windows at the mind-boggling jobs on offer at the temping agencies: skilled workers are currently being sought, security guards, road sweepers, packers. They jot it all down on scraps of paper. They often linger around Barbès-Rochechouart before walking up Rue Myrha and into the heart of the market.

Then comes the inescapable ritual of reunions. Embraces that seem to go on forever in the middle of stalls piled high with smoked fish, mangoes, guavas and soursops. Full-throated laughter and jostlings without any apology to the victims, even if their toes have been stamped on.

They have their own style when it comes to striking up a conversation:

"Is that you I'm seeing? No, I don't believe it! How are you?"

"Have you seen me even catch flu here?"

"And what about our friend Makaya, what's he up to?"

"He is on a trip back to the home country to test the waters."

"Really?"

"Oh come on, he'd been gathering dust here for fourteen years! In this country white hair falls like snow in the mountains. And you end up having to use Pento hair gel to put people off the scent . . ."

"Do you think he'll come back?"

"In theory, yes, if he's got his wits about him. When the mouse strays too far from his hole, it's a battle to reclaim it! Anyone can leave France without something to fall back on. And the police don't give a monkey's because you're scarpering at your own expense. But coming back to Paris is another story! They'll pick up on it straight away if your face isn't a proper match for the ID you show them!"

"What, you mean he hadn't fixed his papers before leaving?"

"No, the whole point is he went back to buy an ID. He said he'd use the opportunity to lower his age as well so he could carry on living in the hostel for young workers in Châtillon. Because in those hostels, you must be fresh-faced and under twenty-five, but he was thirty-two with a beard so long it reached the ground!"

"So he's going to be a rich man when he comes back with all those IDs! You know him well, tell him to reserve a driving licence for me, I've failed the Highway Code for the past five years."

"You can count on me, he'll do you a good price, he's a childhood friend. We led the wild life together . . ."

* * *

And then there are some compatriots who don't make their way from the Gare du Nord, but from the Gare de l'Est. The Marché Dejean is a detour, but they don't care. They like drifting towards Rue de Strasbourg. They're in no hurry. They know how to ponder time. But they can also pick up the pace when they need to, suddenly turning into crazy dromedaries. They walk along Rue de Strasbourg to soak up the atmosphere of Château d'Eau, the temple of hairdressing and negro cosmetics. There are always crowds in front of the métro station where skanky touts hassle passers-by with Jackson Five bushy hair. They offer them speedy cut-price haircuts in dimly lit basements or on the ninth floor of a nearby dilapidated building with no lift. These touts know how to make prospective customers feel like they have no choice, they lead them down winding corridors and up dark stairwells where the sound of scissors and the sputtering of second-hand clippers can be heard all day long.

Once I came across a character who wasn't from the Congolese milieu – he was Central African. He was just about to cross the road when a tout, licking his lips with relish, pounced on him like a cat jumping on easy prey:

"What is that you've got on your head, my brother? Follow me, we will fix that with two snips of the scissors, a good job, double quick! You won't believe your eyes! You will look like a real Sapper, oh yes, a proper one!"

"No thank you, my brother, I haven't had my hair cut for a long time now, and anyway I . . ."

"What do you mean? So you are happy to stroll around with a crow's nest on top of your head? Did no one tell you that French water is full of limestone, you wouldn't believe how much since the Left fell from power? Look at your shoulders, anyone would think it was snowing every day in your hair! My god, it's people like you who give us a bad name in this country! How can a White lady who is healthy in mind and body even

look at you with hair like that? Come on, I'm giving
you this advice as a brother, don't spoil things for our
race, our people have already suffered too much for
four hundred years!"

The harassed man ended up giving in and following
the tout, who pocketed a commission after making his
sitting duck perch on a dirty chair with legs that were
out of all proportion. He closed the door behind him
and headed off again out into the street in the hope
of harvesting another dazed victim. Now, was the
hairdresser going to attack the frizzy vegetation he was
eyeing scornfully? Was he going to comb it? He was
shilly-shallying. He risked breaking his comb, because
this customer's hair was a dusty, unassailable mop of
dry grass . . .

* * *

Château d'Eau is a place of transit for us before reaching
Château Rouge. There's Luxure, a shop where they sell all
sorts of female wigs that smell of naphthalene and baby
vomit. Girls who want to be on a par with blue-eyed
blondes flock to the shop from morning to night, while
the blue-eyed blondes go there to get their hair braided
so they'll look like Africans.

Sometimes you'll find influential personalities from
our community hanging out in the area to gauge how
well their reputation has taken root. It's a varied line-up
of personalities: businessmen staying in Formule 1

motels on the outskirts of Paris, compulsive liars who claim to be great travellers but are incapable of locating on a map the countries they say they've visited, the legitimate or illegitimate sons of Heads of State, of ministers, of political refugees and opposition members who only represent their ethnic group, international footballers we've never seen playing on the telly, musical stars overtaken by the latest developments in instruments and the proliferation of tracks in recording studios . . .

At Château d'Eau you can find the latest musical hits from both Congos. Traffic wardens and police officers grumble and waste their ink raining down fines on cars parked on main thoroughfares classified as "red". Many of these vehicles have number plates from European countries other than France . . .

One day I spotted a well made-up woman wearing pyjamas and carpet slippers, even though people said she lived in Creil, a banlieue more than fifty minutes from Paris by train. When she was heckled for her attire that was better suited for bed and shut-eye, she replied that France was a country of liberty, equality and fraternity.

"And anyway, you bunch of ignoramuses, haven't you noticed the label on my pyjamas is Yves Saint-Laurent? I didn't buy them for hiding in bed with, they're for people to see! Before opening your mouths, take a good look at who you're dealing with!"

I should point out that they don't just cut hair in

Château d'Eau. They don't just go for cars with foreign number plates. And you won't just find women in carpet slippers and Yves Saint-Laurent pyjamas. There are street hawkers too, peddling clothes. Their deals are sealed in café toilets, despite the beady-eyed complaints of the local traders. And people play cards, with bank notes passing from hand to hand at such a speed they'd push David Copperfield into early retirement.

It is also where I heard the famous speech by one of my compatriots, nicknamed "The Opinion Leader of Château d'Eau", and who has the misfortune to be a permanent scapegoat for the police whenever they're searching the area with a fine-tooth comb.

On this particular day he answered with:

"Officers, if you think that I am an illegal immigrant then you are mistaken! Nothing justifies this stop and search, in as far as I am causing no disturbance of the peace. Moreover, why just me and not the entire neighbourhood? I am not the only person with swarthy looks around here, oh no! You have no right to treat me like this, and I should like to remind you that the Penal Code forbids such public humiliations. I can assure you that I will be writing to the Minister of Justice and to some upstanding people such as your Robert Badinters, your Bernard-Henri Lévys and above all to Professeur Jacquard who takes such matters very seriously! Believe me, this will be discussed on the 8 O'Clock News, and even on Canal Plus. And you're surprised that Château

Rouge is constantly in the national headlines. You flout human rights in a so-called democratic country! The reality is that banana republics aren't always the ones we think they are. Montesquieu himself, in *The Spirit of the Laws*, said that . . ."

The Leader, who was manhandled, made to face the other way and pinned against the wall, was unable to finish his diatribe. The crowd railed against the police while taking the precaution of doing it from the other side of the street.

Once again, The Leader was becoming the hero of the day, his words were repeated in nearby cafés and, later on, in the Marché Dejean at Château Rouge . . .

As I was opening my door I heard someone say hello to me in the corridor. I turned around: it was Mr Hippocratic. What had he been drinking to greet me like that from one day to the next?

Surprised by his change of tune, I said hello back. I went into my studio and switched on the telly: an African president was suspected of having poisoned his opponent. I was instantly reminded of the way in which the President of the big Congo had got rid of his fierce opponent, Moleki Nzela, more than two decades ago. Moleki Nzela was very popular, people said that although living abroad, he was already almost in power because a large European stadium had to be booked whenever he held a meeting. Moleki Nzela's misfortune most likely boiled down to the fact that he had given a Fiat 500 to the most notorious madam in his country, a woman everybody would call "Mama Fiat 500" from then on. It's a piece of history that gets told in every street of both Congos. And if it had happened here in Europe, pupils would have long since been studying it at school.

From time to time Moleki Nzela used to come to

our small Congo, but this opponent had to do so under
cover because our Head of State had links with the
Head of State opposite and the two of them would give
each other end-of-year presents: hand over my bloody
idiot of an opponent who brays to Paris morning, noon
and night, and I'll hand over yours who's playing it up
for Brussels even though he doesn't have hairy testicles.
From one day to the next we found out that Moleki
Nzela had been poisoned by the President opposite.
Now the people in the street held this against the
President, and so the hunt was on for a name that would
suit him better than his clown's glasses. The day after
the murder, the people of the big Congo nicknamed
their Head of State "The King of Fools". There was a
song to spread this appellation. But it was best not to
sing it out loud, for risk of a date with the guillotine.
Alas for the President, the song was being whispered on
everyone's lips, and you could hear people whistling in
the street, like Brassens, the singer from Sète, that there
was little hope of de-throning the King of Fools, and so
this sovereign could sleep soundly at night, everybody
would have to follow him dutifully, it was possible to
topple the Shah of Iran, but there wasn't much chance
of de-throning the King of Fools . . .

The King of Fools hadn't annihilated Moleki Nzela
because of any political disagreement, no, it was a
tale of lust. The President and his opponent were well
acquainted with Mama Fiat 500 who ran the biggest

pleasure business in the country opposite, right in the centre of the district of Matongé, and she kept the high-ranking personalities for herself because, again according to the singer from Sète, you don't wiggle your backside in the same way for a hardware-store owner, a sacristan, or a civil servant, let alone a President for life or an implacable opponent. It was a close run thing as to whether the President opposite and his opponent might bump into each other in front of Mama Fiat 500's door, where each was going to do his business. She knew how to set the timetable, but a traffic jam could mess with all that. Normally the King of Fools would turn up late at night. He came to escape the tantrums of his wife, a real pain in the neck who forced the King of Fools to clean his nails while he was jigging about on top of her even though their whole country, and ours too, knew that she was no Venus.

On the first evening that the King of Fools thought he'd spotted his eternal opponent round at Mama Fiat 500's, he rubbed his eyes in disbelief and turned round several times to face his four fixers crammed into an ordinary car but armed right up to their dental cavities:

"Shit, did you see what I just saw? That man sneaking out by the secret door, over there, on the other side, can you see him? That's Moleki Nzela, my bloody idiot of an opponent who spouts a load of rubbish about me from Belgium!"

The henchmen replied with one voice:

"Oh no, Mr President, Moleki Nzela lives in Brussels. He has been banned from entering this country for seventeen years, we have your presidential decree in our glove compartment."

He glanced at the decree, and recognised his signature:

"That is indeed my signature . . . But all the same, are you sure it wasn't him I just saw?"

"Absolutely certain, Mr President! Moleki Nzela, that son of a bitch, is meant to be sick in Brussels and he can't even pay for his hospital expenses any more, rumour has it that he'd like to call upon your goodwill to honour his bills, which are piling up! Ha! Ha! Ha!"

"Ah, yes, that's right, I have heard that story, I must just be imagining things! That fool will get nothing out of me, let him croak his last over there in Europe! I'd rather pay for his funeral, it would cost the State less."

The henchmen burst out laughing and praised the presidential sense of humour which, according to them, the King of Fools always exercised. They scrupulously noted down what they referred to as "the President's humoristic nuggets".

After a little while, the King of Fools stopped laughing. He returned to the attack, as if suddenly bitten by a mosquito:

"Hold on, hold on, hold on, oh no, oh dearie me no, there's something wrong with this story . . . You're saying it wasn't Moleki Nzela I just saw over there, eh? All right, but a man still got away on the other side, and if it wasn't that bloody idiot of an opponent Moleki Nzela, then tell me who the fugitive was, eh? Isn't that what I pay you for?"

One of the men, the shortest one who always had an answer for everything, tried to calm the King of Fools:

"Mr President, allow me to point out that there are a lot of girls on Mama Fiat 500's plot of land . . ."

"So?"

"It's their trade. And she's their boss."

"So?"

"Just as there are lots of girls, so there are also lots of men who come, who leave, who sneak out by the back door because they need to keep things hush-hush, it's like that every day . . ."

"Yes, but there is only one Mama Fiat 500 inside! And anyway, you get up my nose, you've always got an answer for everything! Well then, shit, that is why you are not tall!"

"Allow me to offer my apologies, Mr President . . ."

"I suppose you think I'm impressed by your degree from Sciences Po?"

"Not at all, Mr President . . ."

"Do you realise that I fought in Indo-China?"

"Of course, Mr President, all the textbooks for our History remind us of this fact . . ."

"Do you realise that there are important people who study my place in the history of political ideas in this world? Do you realise that even de Gaulle and

Pompidou were frightened of me, eh? Do you realise that when I cough France catches the flu, eh?"

"Quite so, Mr President . . ."

"Well, I've had enough of short men like you, tomorrow you're fired! You will hand back your black Mercedes to the presidency, along with your villa by the river! Find me a tall man, you imbecile, and preferably one without a degree from Sciences Po! What I'm asking for right now isn't rocket science: I want to know who that man was who just left my Mama Fiat 500's place, do I make myself crystal clear?"

Seeing as the short man with an answer for everything had gone very quiet and teary-eyed, the tallest of the four ventured:

"Mr President, I don't have a degree from Sciences Po, and I'm tall, one metre ninety-three centimetres as a matter of fact . . . With your permission I would simply like to remind you that your Mama Fiat 500 may be the boss of these girls, but she is yours, and yours alone, Mr President. She only does that thing with you, nobody else may touch her. That said, she does have to eat, to feed herself as it is written in the Constitution that you yourself drew up with wisdom and sagacity, and I quote, if I may be so bold, the sublime Article 15 of our supreme Law: "All citizens, both men and women, must find a way of getting by in life and not wait for help from the founding Father of the Nation . . .""

The King of Fools was startled:

"That is very badly written! Very, very badly written, that Article 15! Are you sure it's in my Constitution by me, that?"

"Yes, it's in your Constitution by you, Mr President. And in addition, Article 17 as modified by . . ."

"All right, all right, you can spare me your opinion of-no-fixed-degree! You sat the exams for all the degrees in France but didn't get a single one, and now you dare open your mouth to talk to me about the modification of my supreme Law? Did I ask for your opinion, eh?"

"No, Mr President . . ."

"Well then, shit, don't open your mouth unless what you have to say is more beautiful than silence! I know my law, because it's my law, and because I am the law!"

"Right you are, Mr President . . .

"Let us return to serious matters: who was the character I saw leaving Mama Fiat 500's place if it wasn't Moleki Nzela, that complete fool of an opponent who criticises me on the cable channels of Europe with the tacit support of the Whites who are jealous of our diamonds and our okapi, eh?"

Another bodyguard shyly took over:

"Mr President, with your permission . . ."

"How tall are you, eh?

"One metre sixty-three centimetres, but I get up to one metre sixty-seven centimetres when I wear the Salamander shoes they sell in the Lebanese shops in the centre of town . . ."

"What have you got to say on the subject of this man who vanished on our approach?"

"As a matter of fact, Mama Fiat 500 has a little business going with the girls . . ."

"And what has that got to do with anything?"

"What I mean is, there are other customers who come for these other girls . . ."

"I still don't see the connection!"

"These customers have to go in to Mama Fiat 500's private sitting room . . ."

"What for?"

"To pay for their session, they don't pay the girls directly, they pay the boss and . . ."

"Hold on, hold on, hold on a minute . . . You're not as stupid as I thought, you're the best!"

"Thank you, Mr President . . ."

"So you're saying that the character who just left is a customer who came for another girl, not for my Mama Fiat 500 who's mine?"

"Exactly so, Mr President . . ."

"Well, that does indeed change everything!"

"Mr President, we should be discreet and not hang about even if we are in an unmarked car, either we've got to leave or you've got to go and find your Mama Fiat 500 . . ."

"This is true . . . But how did I never notice you were so talented before?"

"Because my other colleagues are taller than me, and

it's hard to see me especially when I always walk behind them . . ."

"So why were you hiding how smart you were from me? Why were you letting these other idiots with their foul-smelling mouths do the talking, eh?"

"They are my bosses, Mr President . . ."

"Well from this minute on, you are their boss!"

"Thank you, Mr President . . ."

"I have to go in now."

"Please do, Mr President, we will guarantee your cover as usual . . ."


A few days later, when the King of Fools returned to the premises, with the same henchmen, he witnessed the same scene being played out. It was indeed Moleki Nzela who had managed to return to the country opposite by travelling via our country. The four men were first of all dismissed for offences against national security, then eliminated without trial.

From now on four new hefty guards accompanied the King of Fools to Mama Fiat 500's with, as their secondary mission, laying a trap for Moleki Nzela.

Just as Moleki Nzela was coming out of Mama Fiat 500's shack, two henchmen grabbed him, immobilised him and forced him to swallow hemlock.

"At least he'll die a philosopher's death," remarked one of the henchmen.

The news that did the rounds in the country opposite

was clear: Moleki Nzela was dead following a long illness in a Brussels hospital. The President in his boundless generosity, the press release pointed out, would pay for his funeral and promote this worthy son of the country to the rank of Hero of the Revolution . . .

* * *

I switched off the telly and the light, and fell asleep thinking about how the new opponent who had just been murdered in Africa would also be promoted to the rank of Hero of the Revolution because "the dead are all brave men", as the singer from Sète would have said . . .

# IV

My surprises with Mr Hippocratic weren't over yet. He knocked on my door to invite me to the Roi du Café. He had, he added, something very important to tell me.

I followed him because I could still hear Louis-Philippe advising me to reach out to him. Not that I could see what we had to say to each other. So I let Mr Hippocratic do the talking just as I let our Arab on the corner do the talking.

We sat inside, at a spot that wasn't far from the terrace. Mr Hippocratic couldn't keep still, he seemed to have a case of ants in his pants.

He cleared his throat and began:

"I am not against you, that is why I have invited you here today . . . I had a bad dream about you. A car ran you over at the Gare du Nord and everybody walked past your body without stopping. I was passing by, I lifted you onto my shoulders so I could drive you to Lariboisière. But it was too late, there was too much blood, and you died in my arms . . . I cried for the first time in my life. I don't want to go to heaven thinking I'm the cause of your death. So I'm asking for your forgiveness, yes, I'm asking you to forgive me for everything I've done to you. And if you die today or tomorrow, remember it's got nothing to do with me, I've covered myself with a *mea culpa* . . . That said, I would also like you to find out who I am and what I think, because I know that you are going to die soon, my dreams always come true in the end. I'm a good person, and an upright citizen, my skin isn't too black, and my nose isn't too squashy. In my opinion, small minds exaggerate the injustice done to Africans when to this day your man in black Africa lives in a state of barbarism and savagery that prevents him from being part and parcel of civilisation. Now take me, I love France, I'm a big fan of white women and pig's trotters, so please understand my anger, it's not directed against you but against all the Blacks who criticise colonisation. You're not like them, it's taken me a long while to realise this, I was very wrong to give you such a hard time. Do you fully appreciate that without colonisation you wouldn't have had blondes, redheads and pig's trotters, eh? Come on now, let's be honest about this!"

A waiter came by with two coffees. Mr Hippocratic looked daggers at him, as if he had committed a crime against humanity.

"Waiter! What are you serving me here? I asked for a cognac, not wild cat's piss! I've been coming here for years, have you ever seen me drink that stuff?"

The waiter shook his head. He appeared to have got the measure of Mr Hippocratic's temperament. He came back with a cognac.

"And where are my ice?"

"You usually take your cognac without ice, monsieur . . ."

"Well, today I want ice!"

While the waiter went to find some ice, Mr Hippocratic leaned in towards me:

"Did you see that waiter? I'll have him fired, I swear! His hair's a bit fuzzy, I wouldn't be surprised if he had negro blood somewhere! Take a good look at him, is it normal to employ people like that, eh?"

The waiter put the ice on the table.

"You won't be getting a tip today!" Mr Hippocratic called out after him.

Then he downed his cognac in one before carrying on:

"I hear that some ungrateful Blacks are seeking reparations for the losses caused by colonisation. Come, come. Let us not pick the wrong battle. I say there is much to be gained from the legacy of colonisation. What is colonisation, eh? It is a movement of generosity, it is aid for the small nations in darkness! Do you understand? Civilised beings went to help the savages who were living in trees and scratching themselves with their toes. The natives used to eat each other, without even adding salt to their human flesh! Is that a normal way to behave? In fact, my favourite colonisers are the Belgians. They didn't mess about, those Belgians! To

understand this properly, you need to take a close look
at the photos of the natives in the Belgian Congo during
the blessed era of the colonies. And let me tell you,
they are magnificent! What artistry! There are chopped
hands. There are shaved heads. It was the Belgians
who invented the number-one haircut, because they
wouldn't tolerate fuzzy hair. It was all positive, but the
natives could only see the down side. And when the
Belgians got annoyed, well, they chopped off the natives'
hands and shaved their heads without any other form
of trial! Which was only to be expected, considering the
natives talked too much without saying anything. They
bring you light, they bring you civilisation and other
knick-knacks, and you lot still dare to make a fuss in
your pidgin French. At the very least you could have
said: "Thank you, Bwana! Thank you, Bwana! Thank
you, Bwana!" On top of which, those natives were now
learning how to pronounce the word *Independence*. But
it was the glasses of Patrice Lumumba and Co. that
irritated the Belgians most of all, which is why they were
keener on that brave sergeant Mobutu who entered the
Pantheon of the century's Great Men. Thanks to what?
To colonisation, by Jove! Now listen here, just a few days
ago I was thinking about how serious the situation was
becoming. Luckily we voted in a brilliant law, which
enhances the status of colonisation. There was no point
in waiting for acknowledgement like that to come from
those ungrateful Negroes! They are so black that they

blacken everything, even those truths that leap out at you. I say that the African leaders should be inspired by this law, which restores the glory of colonisation. For example, a banana republic could promulgate a law that recognises the benefits of Idi Amin Dada's dictatorship, of Mobutu's one-party system, of torture in the death camps of Sékou Touré, etc. Isn't that brilliant, eh? And I'm only talking to you about dead dictators here. I don't want any trouble with the ones who are still alive . . ."

"Now look, much as . . ."

"No, this is a serious problem, very serious! You're going to die soon, you've got to listen to me! I said come and have a drink with me because this way you'll know I'm not speaking out against you. I don't want you talking nonsense to the Lord above. So don't interrupt me whatever you do, I won't stand for it! You've always taken me for a fool, and a racist too I imagine. Do I complain about the fact it was you Africans who sold the West Indians to the Whites, eh? Did the Whites know where to go to find the Blacks in the bush, eh? No, they relied on village chiefs saying to them: come, there are fine strong Blacks at such a place, they'll make good slaves! That's the trouble with slavery! Why don't you ever talk about these Blacks who aided and abetted the Whites, eh? Why don't you ever talk about the Arabs who were also involved in slavery over there, eh? Leave the West in peace! Let people stop blaming us Europeans, enough is enough when it comes to the tears of the white man, Europe forever accused, and the innocence of the people of the Third World! They've taken away our right to tell the Blacks what we think of them, even though the Blacks don't hold back when it comes to criticising the Whites instead of getting on with the work of developing their continent. Is this how you want to go down in History, eh? This isn't about dressing the way you like or playing your tom-toms every Sunday. I'm talking about the history of colonisation, the one that doesn't get explained properly to people even though without colonisation you wouldn't be where you are today. So I don't wish to be referred to as being black any more. I don't want people to keep saying things like Blacks are naturally strong, handsome, sporty, they've got stamina, they age better than Whites, etc. Let's be absolutely clear about this, what have you got that the Whites haven't, eh? An over-sized penis? Is that it? Is that all? Come, come, it's all screwed up on that level too. Sex was your private preserve to impress the blondes and the redheads. But you lost this advantage when a writer gave away all your secrets in his book. He explained that Blacks weren't always as well hung as all that. The upshot of which is that blondes and redheads in search of negroes now know that the over-sized penis of Black men is just a tall story, like the one about little boys being born in the cabbage patch. There are even rumours that some Whites have got bigger ones than you lot. Can you see the problem? . . . Listen, it wasn't so long ago that you desperate negroes relied on the slave trade as a source of revenue. Because it gave you lots of reasons to snivel, to tell those Whites they were nothing but big bad wolves. There were small groups of negroes who even demanded reparations left right and centre to the point of sullying the Place de la Bastille, in that very place where our people fought to maintain our dignity. My God, this story of slavery and the negro slave trade is over. In fact it's been done and dusted in my head, ever since a black writer – what's his name again? – said you negroes didn't have white hands, that you were just a bunch of hypocrites. You're guilty, you were accessories to crime and all the rest. Oh yes, his book was *Bound to Violence*, but I've forgotten the writer's name, it's a very African name, I'm sure it'll come back to me after another cognac . . ."

I was wondering where Mr Hippocratic was heading with these random musings. I couldn't get a word in edgeways. So I decided to let him pour his heart out, given it seemed full to bursting.

He ordered another glass.

"I know what's going through your head right now. You're thinking: 'This man's completely crazy!' Well, don't be so quick to judge me, I'm only saying what I think and what I see. Colonisation was all positive, I'm telling you. Without colonisation, would you have had the Senegalese soldiers? Would you have known what a pith helmet was, eh? I'm not as ignorant as you think. I know a bit about Africa, I buy books from the Rideau Rouge. And what do I remember from what I've read? A dazzling truth: it's thanks to colonisation that the Cameroonian Ferdinand Oyono wrote *The Old Man and the Medal* and *Houseboy*; it's thanks to colonisation that another Cameroonian, Mongo Beti, wrote *Cruel Town* and *The Poor Christ of Bomba*; it's thanks to colonisation that the Guyanan René Maran wrote *Batouala* and for the first time a Black won the Prix Goncourt which is meant to be the reserve of Whites, that's right! Do you think if it wasn't for colonisation we would have given as prestigious a prize as the Goncourt to a Black writer who, in addition, criticised us in his book even though he was working in our colonial administration? Which only goes to show the settlers were very generous, that's fair play for you, but while they accepted criticism no dialogue is tolerated by your dictators. If colonisation hadn't existed, your Shaka Zulu would have invented it. And he wouldn't have overlooked the whip, derision, rape, pillaging, the exploitation of man by animal and the extermination of the tribes of the Belgian Congo. Shaka Zulu would also have decreed that the whole of Zaire be his private property, just as the Belgian Leopold II did! Oh I know, I know, yes I know there's that other one, that Aimé Césaire, he wanted to ruin everything for colonisation in his book which I've also got at home and which only has fifty-nine pages in tiny print and which was published in 1955 by Présence Africane over there, I mean in the 5th arrondissement, 25 *bis* Rue des Ecoles, Métro Cardinal Lemoine or Maubert-Mutualité, depending which side you're coming from and what you're looking for. *Discourse on Colonialism*, that's the title of the book I'm talking about! I never want to read it again or all my anger against those negroes will come back when I've decided I don't want anything more to do with them. I mean it really wasn't very nice of Césaire to hold forth like that for fifty-nine pages in tiny print making all the Whites who read it shortsighted. Why, it's even ungrateful to write the sort of things he wrote. Do you realise that he wrote, black on white, the following – I've memorised it: 'What am I driving at? At this idea: that no one colonises innocently, that no one colonises with impunity either; that a nation which colonises, that a civilisation which justifies colonisation - and therefore force - is already a sick civilisation, a civilisation that is morally diseased, that irresistibly, progressing from one consequence to another, one repudiation to another, calls for its Hitler, I mean its punishment'. Stuff and nonsense! Where did he find those turns of phrase? That Césaire won't make me change my ideas. Colonisation was useful. Let me talk to you about it in my own words! You didn't have any Blacks commanding you back then. Which was better than being commanded by those black Kings who burped and farted after eating. The African salaries of functionaries were paid on time. The White man was carried to the next village on a chair made of animal skin. It was the most comfortable method of transport. Why condemn the poor man, eh? In his place, I'd have let myself be carried on a chair by a dozen muscular negroes too. A vehicle? Let's be level-headed about this! How were vehicles going to get through those jungles, eh? Between two rutting hippopotamuses? Don't give me such rubbish! Drink your coffee, or it'll get cold . . ."

Sure enough, my coffee had gone cold. Mr Hippocratic noticed my attention waning, I was more interested in a girl who was sitting out on the terrace.

"That is the drama of the African!" declared Mr Hippocratic, pointing to the girl.

He stood up and went over to say something to her. He stayed for more than five minutes, doing all the talking.

When he came to sit back down again, he seemed vexed.

"Did you see what she was about to do, that half-caste? Well, she was going to light a cigarette! I told her not to do it or else to leave the premises. I mean, who does she think she is? Right, now where was I? Ah yes, colonisation . . . You were beaten about a bit, but it was for your own good. At school you were banned from speaking your barbarian languages in the playground. Civilisation or barbarism, you had to choose, because black nations and culture were incompatible. You were being offered civilisation! So Jules Ferry's free primary schooling was copper-bottomed. It marked the end of pidgin grammar, for example: 'the banana me is eating' was replaced with 'da banana me eat'. Enough was enough, thanks to colonisation. Your forefathers had become Gauls too. And those Gauls made their magic potion with the help of your oil, seeing as you were stupid and gullible. So the settler took that black gold to refine it. Well, come on, wasn't this in your own interests? And, between you and me, life working as a houseboy for a settler was better than a strange destiny as a hunter or a fetish man. The colonial town wasn't as cruel as all that. You shouldn't believe what your intellectuals have told you. And not only that but when you people grew old and you'd given up your children to go and fight for France in Europe, you were eligible for a medal which you received from the Cercle Commander. Do you think medals are just given out willy-nilly? It's all positive, I'm telling you. The negroes didn't have anything before the Whites arrived. It was empty, chaos, anarchy, nothing in Timbuktu, no Malian Empire, no soul, no culture, no Gods, no religion, no political or social structure! They had to choose for their survival: a black skin or a white mask. And the cleverest among them chose the white mask because black skin is the curse of Ham. Do you see the problem? I'm going to stop now, but you need to know that I'm not railing against you, I don't like people who are ungrateful, I'm just saying things the way they are. Afterwards, you can take my words or toss them into the bins down in our basement where we often run into each other, it's up to you. It was all positive, I'm telling you. From now on, since you're going to die soon, let us bury the hatchet, come and see me if you want to discuss some of these issues before your death, but let us live in peace. I know everything about you, your woman, your child and that man who played the tom-toms. That's not a problem, that's life. Find yourself another woman, preferably a white one instead of clinging to your original colour . . ."

He took out a note from his wallet and put it down on the table. The waiter gave him ten centimes in change, which Mr Hippocratic immediately pocketed:

"I made it clear there would be no tip for you, so why are you standing in front of me like a moron?"

* * *

As we were leaving the café Mr Hippocratic said to me:

"I remember now: the name of that African who wrote *Bound To Violence* is Yambo Ouologuem. You should read it, he at least was a proper gentleman. That's why everybody ganged up against him . . ."

**I**t happened at Jip's when the other pals hadn't showed up yet. I wasn't in the mood to talk because I was on my way back from Porte de la Chapelle where I'd done a Western Union to pay the maintenance allowance to the home country. I ordered a beer and a man who was sitting at the back of the bar got up and made his way over to me. He said he was Breton, that he liked Africa, that in fact all Bretons liked Africa. He was a fan of B-sides too, so we watched the girls going by and I explained to him how to tell the character of this or that girl just by watching her backside move. All of a sudden we switched topics and landed on politics instead of getting a nice eyeful, as groups of Italian and American girls passed by.

I told him there are spies everywhere, and that's why I hate discussing politics in a bar with people I don't know.

"Do I really look like a spy?"

I looked at him closely, he was the spitting image of the Thompson Twins in *Tintin*. Same baldness, same moustache, same dark suit. He bought me two rounds of Pelfort.

"I simply want to know what you Africans make of

our politics and to find out how things happen where you come from."

I have a feeling this man will remember me for the rest of his life. I've never talked for as long in a bar sat opposite a stranger. I don't give a monkey's if he was a spy, what I said came from the bottom of my heart ...

* * *

When I told the Breton that I was from the Congo, the tiny Congo, a patch of land measuring three hundred and forty-two thousand square kilometres with a window that gives onto the Atlantic Ocean and a river that ranks amongst the biggest in the world, a country that should on no count be confused with the Congo opposite which is bigger and which used to be the private property of the King of the Belgians, he didn't agree with me:

"Pah, historically the two Congos were part of the same territory, let's not make a whole song and dance about it!"

I paused for a moment. And then I said, NO, NO, NO, you mustn't muddle up the two countries or I'll lose my temper. I know only too well that the borders separating us are the result of a carving up between France and Belgium because these two nations would have ripped each other's guts out if there hadn't been a conference in Berlin to calm their belligerent moods. I don't want to hear about any of that! I wasn't there when the French and the Belgians were calling each

other every name under the sun across the banks of our
river. And you weren't there either, Mr Breton! I have
my country of origin, and the Congolese opposite have
theirs, there are borders, end of story. I don't want any
confusion on that front. Everybody must stay on his
own plot of land and cultivate his own garden. Your
ancestors know why they decided there should be
borders between our two Congos. It's not for me to
contradict their scheming. I am very angry with the big
Congo because they reverted to the name of Congo
when they had already decided their country would be
called Zaire, whereas we stuck with Congo all along, so
that makes things even more confusing when I am
faced with people who know nothing about the
geography of the region and I have to clarify that I
come from the smaller of the two Congos, not to
mention the fact that all their whores come and work in
our country where they have imported the Horizontal
Revolution. You have no idea what I'm talking about
when I say the Horizontal Revolution. Can you believe
that it is these women from the big Congo who are
governing us right now? That they're the ones who
determine our purchasing power, our pensions, the
distribution of dividends for our oil and the nature of
our foreign policy? Did you know that important
historians have published theses in which they maintain
that this massive migration by ladies of pleasure from
the country opposite towards our country was due to

the good health of our money, the CFA Franc, a well rated currency in the bush, and one that is stronger than the currency of the big Congo, which also used to be called the zaire? Theirs was a real monkey currency, it dropped in value with every hair-brained rumour of a coup d'état, of their Finance Minister's acute gonorrhoea or of the death of their president for life whose austere face, big clown-like glasses, walking stick and leopard-skin headgear could be admired on every bank note. They, meaning the people from the country opposite, were obsessed with calling everything zaire: their huge country, their currency, their whores, their river and everything that couldn't be named while they waited for their President with the austere face to trace back the genealogical tree of his tribe and unearth a pithecanthrope whose unpronounceable name they would borrow in order to rename by presidential decree either a boulevard in the town centre, or a roundabout leading to the embassies of France, the United States or Belgium, but never a dead-end place in a popular district whose streets bear no name, and whose roads don't all lead to Rome. And since in our little country we didn't have enough room to lodge these myriads of women who crossed the river in their canoe-loads, to come to us with their belongings on their heads, so it was that this transhumance brought about the Horizontal Revolution, one that was within the reach of every wallet, and we had masses of women, a whole spate of them, at knock-down prices. Do you see how things came about, eh? We would have preferred a different kind of revolution, but we were aware that the other revolutions, which were all the rage around the world, ended up being too expensive for the people. In any case, given that our State coffers were empty at the very beginning of the Horizontal Revolution, pillaged down to the last centime by the government and the local official liquidator who always paid his own salary in cash first, we would never have had the financial means to give ourselves a revolution in the style of 1789 which you French haven't yet finished picking up the tab for because there are still privileges here, taxes with features that ruin the people of ordinary means, in short inequalities that make everybody laugh who reads The Declaration of Human and Citizen X's Rights. With a bit more political courage, we could have bought ourselves a revised and corrected version of the French Revolution, and France herself would gladly have handed it over to us with immediate effect, offering twenty-four-seven customer service and a Freefone number in the event of the revolution breaking down at night and nobody in the country being able to change the nuts and bolts or replace the dud bulbs caused by a surge in the lights! So all right, that way we would have had our own 1789. But then what, eh? That revolution would have been a luxury product for us. It would have required a longer preparation period, and a shifting of mindsets. We'd have had to find a local Napoleon Bonaparte, for example, whose mission would have been to stage, ten years after 1789, a small Coup d'Etat of 18 Brumaire fomented from the residence of a lady with big buttocks the way I like them, a lady who would also have been called Joséphine de Beauharnais. And then, you can't have a revolution without ideas. So, on that front too, we'd have had to come up with a legacy of revolutionary ideas for future generations so they wouldn't take us for full-time fools who'd been lucky enough to grasp a revolution in their hands but who hadn't bust a gut when it came to the ideas to go with it. But who would have sacrificed themselves for ideas as well as being prepared to die for them when, as your great singer with the moustache says, by forcing the pace of things too much you might die for ideas that don't matter the next day? As a result, without a 1789 that would have been too costly for our plebian pockets and which you would have refused to sell us even on credit because we've got a reputation for never paying off our debts but of going cap in hand to the United Nations and begging shamelessly for them to be cancelled, pure and simple, our small Congo first inherited the Red Revolution which the Russians were selling half-price, in the Marxist-Leninist version, and then, a bit later on and most importantly, the free Horizontal Revolution with the women from the country opposite who set themselves up on every street corner and made our papas lose their heads. Our authorities realised that the aforementioned Horizontal Revolution was of no small consequence and that it had an unfair advantage over the real one, the authentic Red Revolution of our country which many years ago had fallen into the boiling pot of communism without Soviets or electricity, of the dialectics of pure hard knocks, of the kolkhozes and the sovkhozes, of socialism that was more or less scientific, of materialism that was roughly historical. And even our president at the time, the one who didn't wear clown's glasses or leopard skin headgear, His Most High Excellency Meka Okangama, was a pain in the neck with his daily messages for those enslaved to hunger, for the proletarians waiting for goodness knows what in order to unite while making do with factory line work when the Red Revolution was meant to be there for the final struggle, for a world in which there would no longer be employees but just bosses with big bellies and Cuban cigars clamped between their lips. Did you know that already during that time, in order to counter the Horizontal Revolution that was turning up at our borders, our president would only swear on long passages taken from a tome by Engels – pronounced by him as "Angel" – a book entitled *Ludwig Feuerbach and the End of Classical German Philosophy*, a book he was never without as if he had written it himself? These were real political moments, Mr Breton! I'm not kidding with this story,

even if I am a bit drunk! When our Marxist president
was on form, the sweat dripping from his bulging
forehead, his tie badly knotted like a suicidal who'd
finally managed to hang himself, he would lay into the
whole lot of your philosophers from Antiquity, that
bunch of lechers who were too quick to extol life's
pleasures such as premature ejaculation and
masturbation with the help of boa grease, who didn't
worry about anything except their beard and who quite
possibly, between two slapdash lessons in the Agora,
did the business with pretty mummified girls barely out
of puberty. Our president did not forget to denounce
your vagabonds from the past who lived in barrels, were
stupid enough to light hurricane lamps in broad
daylight and didn't even have it in them to whet our
enthusiasm, to offer us a unanimous definition of
philosophy, a definition that would at least have had
the eternal merit of exempting young secondary school
students from splitting hairs during their end-of-year
exams when they run down their pens answering
perennial questions such as: "What is Philosophy?"
This is not a topic to joke about, Mr Breton! Our
President had read a lot even if he didn't have his
primary school certificate and peeled potatoes in the
kitchens of the French army during the Second World
War. Like all dictators, he knew his classics, looked
down his nose at the moderns whom he reproached for
having abandoned the imperfect subjunctive from one

day to the next in exchange for a language that had more freedom but was inevitably less elegant. And it was by drawing on his general culture, for which his people envied him, that he also presented us with *Capital* by Karl Marx, just after citing Engels – and the scandal-spreaders concluded that the President was very fond of the books of Marx and his wife Angel. His Most High Excellency wasn't just anybody, and you should know that, you French! In his opinion your visionary men from bygone eras, also known as philosophers, had simply interpreted the world, but from now on it needed changing with Rwandan machetes and Kalashnikovs imported directly from Russia via the narrow border with Cabinda even if the Angolans and their rebels didn't agree . . .

The Breton paid the bill and said goodbye. Willy who had been half-listening to us came over and whispered to me:

"I think you need to go home now. In all the time I've known you, I've never heard you rant like this. You made that poor Breton, who looked like a very nice man, feel uncomfortable. He won't be paying us another visit any time soon . . ."

# Epilogue
# A Year and a Half Later

A year and a half already . . .

I'm not dead despite Mr Hippocratic being convinced I would be. Quite the opposite, in fact, some good things have been happening in my life.

I'm a different man now, and it makes my friends at Jip's laugh when they see me wearing my seventies' style flares.

"So you've dropped the Sappe, and you're turning hippie now?" teased Lazio the security guard.

"Buttologist, you're heading for the loony-bin," concluded Yves the just-Ivorian.

\* \* \*

I straighten my hair and pull it back in the style of the films from the thirties and forties that I watch with Sarah. She likes me this way, I've got to stand out, to create my own look even if it means going against the tide. It's time-consuming because I have to track down the right products to a shop in Château d'Eau. Sometimes the shop-keeper is out of stock, and I have to wait for weeks on end with frizzy hair. While I'm waiting for the shop-keeper to get these products in from the United States, I avoid looking at myself in the mirror. When I go out I wear a hat to cover my hair.

A Gabonese man who was hanging around in front of McDonald's at the Gare de l'Est made it clear how pathetic he thought I was, that if I straightened my hair it was because I was uncomfortable with my own negritude, that I had a serious problem, that I brought shame on the finest race in the world, the one that is the origin of everything on earth. It wasn't like I had to give him the time of day since I was waiting for Roger the French-Ivorian who was going to let me have *Right To Veto*, the latest album from Koffi Olomide. But seeing as the Gabonese man wouldn't stop staring at me, I nodded at him thinking that perhaps he admired my new style of dressing.

He didn't reply but pulled a horrified face:

"I'm not answering! And you know why!"

So I told him where to go, I tried out a saying on him that I'd read somewhere and which sprang to mind: man is the baker of his own life. So it's up to me to knead my body, to transform it the way I understand it, end of story. Why was he sticking his nose in? For one thing I don't whiten my skin, so by rights the Gabonese man should be happy because I know plenty of Blacks who don't hold back from doing that kind of thing to their faces with products imported by Original Colour's former Nigerian lady friends.

The Gabonese man added that I was just a poor Black who didn't like cassava and that I straightened my hair to look like Whites.

"Take a look at yourself, anyone would take you for a monkey! Is this straight-hair business to make you look like a White or something? I see that colonisation continues to wreak havoc on our community!"

I burst out laughing because he was dressed like a bushman with his tie that resembled a penguin's small intestines. He must have been one of those students who are still enrolled even though their white hairs are making them snowy-headed. Who did he think he was, eh?

I decided not to wait around for Roger the French-Ivorian who is often an hour late, if not more.

I spat on the ground and left . . .

"That's it, clear off, you lunatic! After your hair, you'll still have your skin to whiten, and don't forget your elbows, your heels and your knees!"

"**For too long Europe** has force-fed us with lies and bloated us with pestilence. Do you know which black poet said those courageous things, my African brother? We must be honest in life, and say things to people's faces. Take me, have I ever hidden anything from you? Don't I tell you everything? So why did you do it to me, eh? I thought of you as a member of my own family. But you lied to me, you have lied to me ever since the beginning. Now I know that you're like some of the other people in this neighbourhood, you think I'm just a poor Arab on the corner, that my life is played out behind this counter, that I'm worthless. Well, you've got another think coming! What kills me is that today I feel betrayed by a brother from the continent. You've always said that your wife and your child were on holiday in the Congo, haven't you? Well it's a lie!!! What kind of holidays last for over a year and a half? I know about everything. But if the Caribbean gentleman in your building hadn't revealed the truth to me, would I have known these things, eh? How would I have guessed that it was your artist cousin who left with your woman and the little girl, eh? And what does that make me look like in this story, given that I used to say how respectful that man was? And another thing, you've changed, look at you wearing these hoodlum trousers, when you used to dress like the son of a minister! What are you doing straightening your hair, are you ashamed of yourself? And why don't you come to my shop any more? I saw you yesterday with a White girl going to buy toilet paper from the Chinese when I've got stacks of it here. Is that any way to behave towards an African brother? If the Chinese shopkeepers have become powerful it's because they've got more money than we have, it's because people like you make them even more powerful by going to buy toilet paper from them when I've got stacks of it in my shop. Anyway, that is something I can still close my eyes to, but to hide the truth from me, no, no, no! And who is that White girl who comes in and out of your building with you, is that how we're going to achieve the African Unity of our Guide Mouamar Gaddafi? When I was talking about R-E-S-P-E-C-T, you weren't listening to me. Deep down, don't you think that cousin of yours deserved to live with your woman? As I told you, I found him respectful, he wouldn't have done what you've done to me ..."

* * *

The girl our Arab on the corner is talking about is Sarah. She's Belgian on her father's side and French on her mother's. She paints scenes of daily life in bars and cafés, and she says that Château Rouge and Château d'Eau provide plenty of inspiration for her work. At the beginning she made my pals laugh because they didn't realise you could earn your crust by painting cans of beer and Black characters dozing off in front of their glasses.

The day she walked into Jip's we all got that it was the first time she'd set foot in there. She came over to us and said she was looking for someone who would pose for her. Preferably someone flamboyant.

"A bit like you," she added, pointing at me.

My pals all laughed. Paul from the big Congo whispered that the White woman just wanted to get a negro in the sack. Yves the just-Ivorian was eyeing her greedily and drooling:

"Did you see her butt? It's like the gazelles back home in Abidjan. I bet she's already had a Negro whipping it and he's just ditched her, that's why she's come looking for another one who'll take over from him because a White girl can't have a B-side like that unless a good Negro's already worked hard on it. And anyway, what about the will of the people, eh? She's got to be made to pay for the cruel treatment inflicted on us by her ancestors during colonisation. Seeing as she's French-Belgian, both France and Belgium need to cough up. It'll be a double indemnity. What you call killing two birds with one stone . . ."

Willy changed the music because the choral singing he'd brought back from Brazzaville was sending us to sleep and reminding us of those we'd lost. Olivier had already started sobbing.

We knew Willy wanted to dance salsa with this girl, because he put on a Compay Segundo track when he'd rejected our earlier requests to change his funeral music.

He said to Sarah:

"I'm Willy, I'm boss of everything in this bar, and I'm lighter than a sparrow's feather! When I dance I always take my partner higher than the seventh heaven, but rest assured I bring her back to earth very smoothly. Come on sweetheart, this is where the action is, and I'm the best salsa dancer around, the others are just first-class time-wasters. Can I pour you a little glass of ginger to get the engine going?"

Bosco the Embassy Poet was already quoting *The Lake* by Lamartine to her. He went over to the girl and whispered to her: "A single being is missing and the whole world feels deserted." When he wanted to follow this up with *The Sleeper in the Valley*, everybody booed.

Lazio the security guard looked even more muscular than before. You'd have thought he'd gone and rubbed oil into his biceps to impress Sarah. His shaved head was glowing and he flashed a smile that oozed confidence.

The Embassy Poet confided in Paul from the big Congo:

"If that hunk goes out with the girl, I'll start body-building tomorrow!"

And Lazio was whizzing around, proving that he was the one who was boss of everything at Jip's, not Willy, not even the owner Jeannot who'd gone on a road-trip to Morocco with his friends that particular week.

Lazio grabbed the girl in the small of her back, he didn't beat about the bush, he even promised to marry her while Pierrot the White stood back and signalled to me to get in on the action.

I took a few steps, rescued the girl from Lazio's clutches and told her I'd really like to see her paintings, that if she was looking for a model I was happy to give it a go. Her face lit up and, from then on, she directed everything she said at me.

She tried to save face:

"When I said flamboyant just now, I hope I didn't offend you, I meant it in the artistic sense of the term . . ."

I told her that I wasn't at all offended, that flamboyance was an art, that if I understood her it was because I myself had been writing ever since I'd had a writer friend, Louis-Philippe, who was also into art.

She added:

"A writer is an artist too, he paints with his words . . ."

She wanted to paint me at my place, in front of my typewriter, in the middle of all my piles of paper. I gave her my telephone number. She drank a glass of tomato juice and thanked me before leaving.

I heard Willy hectoring me from the counter:

"Buttologist, you stole my dance! If you think that girl's serious, you're mistaken. She'll go looking for another flamboyant type at the Baiser Salé. She's the kind of chick who solicits men in bars, and I know what I'm talking about . . .!"

* * *

Sarah turned up at my place three days later. It was the first time I didn't hear Mr Hippocratic reacting behind his door, probably because of the ceasefire after his speech at the Roi du Café.

I'd tidied everything up at home, but Sarah wanted it to look a bit messy, so I wouldn't be creating a false impression. She asked me why I'd gone to so much trouble doing the housework, tidying my suitcases into one corner and burning incense in the room. I told her I hadn't had anyone back to mine for a while. As I said this, Rose suddenly flashed into my mind. But I brushed her away.

Sarah asked me to stand near the window and she stared at me for a long time before she began drawing me. She did a lot of rubbing out, she kept changing the angle, she told me to look up and to the left for the light. Did she realise I was glancing down too much because I wanted to get a good look at her B-side?

* * *

After she'd done her work we went for a drink at the Roi du Café. Seeing as I felt relaxed chatting with her, I ended up talking a lot about Original Colour and my daughter.

"I'm the father of that little girl, and I won't give up!"

I railed against the Hybrid, his music, his tom-toms and his concerts. She looked me straight in the eye without interrupting me. Then I felt bad about taking up more that my fair share of the conversation.

She stood up without uttering a word and said goodbye. I watched her going down the steps into the métro at Marx-Dormoy. She turned around and smiled at me.

Later on, in the middle of the evening, she called me to say she'd had a nice time, and to thank me for being so open. I didn't notice the time passing, we spent more than two hours on the telephone.

She came back the following week with a picture that was all wrapped up. The portrait she painted of me is hanging on my studio wall now. You can't miss it . . .

like Sarah's paintings. The colours are vibrant. She knows how to express the joy and despair of the characters from Château Rouge and Château d'Eau. I can see her becoming a high-profile painter in the years to come. Her parents are good people. Her father lives in Pantin and runs a printing works and her mother is a beautician in Rambouillet. They adore their only daughter, unlike Original Colour's parents who never want to see their offspring again. The father doesn't say much. Sometimes I play pétanque with him when we go to visit. Her mother, who's more chatty, often asks me for news from the Congo. And seeing as I don't have anything particular to tell her, she keeps saying to me:

"Above all, you must never forget your own country, never . . ."

\* \* \*

Sarah often talks to me about the painter René Magritte whose mother drowned herself when he was fourteen.

One day I said to her:

"So when it comes to painting, you just need to go

to the École des Beaux-Arts, learn the right techniques, and . . ."

She cut me off, looked at me pityingly and answered with:

"What are you saying? True painting transgresses all norms. Magritte himself said: 'A painter doesn't paint to put colour on his canvas, any more than a poet writes to put words on a page.'"

My jaw dropped, because that René Magritte had foreseen all the arguments in order to stand his ground! Perhaps that's what every artist should do before kicking the bucket. Don't leave the business of defining your creativity to others. Toss the keys to your oeuvre here and there if you want to avoid professional pundits making a travesty of your life experience and the sweat of all your labour. I told Louis-Philippe about what Magritte had said the day I introduced him to my new friend. He and Sarah talked on and off about painting, and that's when I found out that Louis-Philippe had a whole collection of paintings by artists from Haiti in his basement. We went down there with torches and spent a long time looking at each canvas and listening to the Haitian writer's commentary. I felt afraid down in that basement, I kept imagining a monster lurking in the dark who would swallow us up in one powerful intake of breath. And anyway those pictures were scary to look at down there. Even the most minor characters seemed to have glowing embers for eyes as well as alligator's teeth. The works where voodoo scenes were depicted made my hair stand on end. Sarah was in seventh heaven, and didn't want to leave. It was when I yawned that Louis-Philippe pointed out:

"There you go, the Congolese and painting is a whole other story! That's why their great Gotene from the Poto-Poto School is dying of hunger and indifference . . ."

As we were walking back up from the basement, I didn't want to be the last in line. You can't be too careful, what with everything I've heard about characters stepping out of painted canvases to slit people's throats.

I made sure I was in between Sarah and Louis-Philippe.

Since then, Louis-Philippe has bought one of Sarah's paintings. It's of a tramp sleeping on the pavement of Rue Riquet, and you can see a bottle of wine poking out of his coat pocket . . .

* * *

Sarah claims I look like a black American jazz musician, Miles Davis. Which explains why I spent an evening studying his photo in a shop that sold cards and photos, not far from the café Au Père Tranquille. I don't know how she came to compare me with him. Probably because of straightening my hair. Of course I salute Miles Davis's genius, even if I don't know his music inside out the way she does. When it comes to people who claim to know a lot about jazz and other hullaballoo music that is supposed to have been invented by black hands like mine, I take their word for it. But to be honest I think I'm cuter than Miles Davis. Sarah goes and adds that the one and only Edith Piaf declared Miles Davis was handsome as a god, that she'd never seen such a beautiful man. Straight up! If Piaf really did say that then all I can think is the kid Edith must have been free and easy with her compliments because I prefer her Marcel Cerdan, world-champion boxer, he was definitely better looking. If Miles Davis had been an ordinary person, meaning without his trumpet and his black hands, would people think of him as a handsome man, eh? I don't think so. When an artist is worshipped, then his fans consider it sacrilege for you to insist he's ugly.

I said to Sarah:

"All Blacks look the same to you . . ."

I watched her going red, and trying to explain that wasn't what she meant, that she wasn't racist in the slightest, look, she was going out with me when there were plenty of Whites in Paris who were chasing after her.

"Your problem is that you're not comfortable in your own skin!" she let out, turning her back on me.

I repeated that I couldn't see any resemblance to Miles Davis. Not only this, but I was convinced that genius was often an excuse for physical ugliness.

"Hold on a moment, he's not ugly, I mean are we really talking about the same person here?"

"I'm telling you, he's ugly!"

I realised that I'd overstepped the mark. That I needed to calm down. That I shouldn't let the demons get the upper hand. I had become a different man. So, to please her, and because I've also come to the conclusion it's best to tell all painters that they have genius, I conceded he was a handsome musician, even though I thought the opposite.

I shouldn't have said that to her because she took me at my word and gave me one of his albums, *Young Miles*. She recommended I listen to "April in Paris" because it was unthinkable for a Parisian not to like that track.

So there she was making me listen to blasts from the trumpet and the clarinet, when I like to listen to Koffi Olomide, Papa Wemba, J-B Mpiana and Werra Son, good stuff from back home that Roger the French-Ivorian gives me from time to time in exchange for me teaching him our language, Lingala.

Our music from back home is something else. And we got rid of the trumpets and other saxophones a long time ago. If you like, there's only Manu Dibango who survived with those instruments. It's all about furious rhythms now. A few lyrics, for one or two minutes tops, and then more than twenty minutes of dance, of "hot stuff". You sweat when you dance, you hold your

partner nice and tight, you try and make her slip up so
she brings her chest and lips right up close. And then,
bam, you're into direct action.

You wouldn't be able to pull off a feat like that with
Miles Davis. But I can't say this to Sarah . . .

* * *

What exasperates me about the kind of music Sarah
likes is that most of the time they don't even sing. I enjoy
lyrics, but this stuff doesn't really have any. Nothing but
cymbals and wind instruments that seem to work her up
into a frenzy. She asks me to surrender to the genius of
Miles Davis, because jazz is stronger than life. Jazz is the
universe. It freed up the minds of ordinary people, she
says, sounding thrilled.

Still, I've been listening to Miles Davis since then.
I'm starting to like his "Venus de Milo". But I've been
careful not to mention this to Sarah, because she prefers
"April in Paris". You mustn't do anything to make Paris
lose its mystique for her . . .

Sarah thinks it's shocking that my friends at Jip's call me Buttologist. So she's nicknamed me "Léon Morin, Priest". She says this is a tribute to Béatrix Beck, a great lady of Belgian literature whose work she subsequently introduced me to because she was annoyed I only read Simenon and the Latin-American novels Louis-Philippe lends me.

"You've got to free yourself up a bit from your fascination with Louis-Philippe! You only read what he tells you to read. Literature doesn't end with Latin America . . ."

She did a good sales pitch on Beck telling me that she had won the Goncourt in 1952 with her *Léon Morin, Priest* which I now recommend my pals read, even if this gets up their nose and makes me sound like a pain in the neck.

\* \* \*

Apart from jazz and Miles Davis, where we don't see eye to eye, I've got to admit it's thanks to Sarah that I've been spending even more time in bookshops recently. I'm reading more books now than all the pairs of Westons, all the Francesco Smalto suits and all the Yves Saint-Laurent ties that I used to wear for my Papa Wemba, Kofi Olomide and J-B Mpiana concerts. I can hold the floor for hours and hours, making people's heads spin with something that's not my sorry story with Original Colour and the Hybrid! Thanks to Sarah, I'm reading a lot of Belgian authors.

One day I turned up at Jip's with a book in my hand, *The Life Of The Bee*. As soon as I appeared in the doorway my pals eyed my book suspiciously, convinced I now had a thing for bees. I sat down in a corner and, since I've decided not to drink alcohol any more because I'm a changed man, I ordered a glass of ginger juice and started reading as if I were alone.

Paul from the big Congo came over to me:

"So you reckon you're some kind of intellectual now that you're with this Sarah girl who paints drunkards and bottles of red wine? What's this book you've come here to read, then?"

"An essay by Maurice Maeterlinck . . ."

"What kind of unpronounceable name is that? Is this writer more famous than Guy des Cars or Gerard de Villiers?"

"He won the Nobel Prize in 1911 . . ."

He looked me up and down before going back to join the others. I heard them trying unsuccessfully to pronounce Maeterlinck, then talking about bees in general, and in particular the ones from Africa. I stood up and left.

Three days later, I came back with a different book. This time it was Yves the just-Ivorian who shouted at me:

"I know how to pronounce the name of your guy who writes about bees!"

I smiled at him. Of course he made a dog's dinner of the Belgian Nobel laureate's name. I noticed he couldn't take his eyes off the book I was holding.

"So what are you reading now after that business with the bees by that . . . Mae . . . Maerink . . . Matae . . . I mean, that Belgian author?"

"Béatrix Beck . . .

"Means nothing to me."

* * *

Sarah has introduced me to the poems of Henri Michaux. But given she couldn't always pick my Belgian authors for me, because there were some books I didn't like, I've clawed myself a bit of freedom.

So I was the one who discovered *Divine Madman* by Dominique Rolin, for example, and that author has fuelled my hang-ups, given I'm still trying to write a book in the style of George Simenon, because he's the Belgian writer I like the most, whatever Sarah thinks.

I'm proud of one thing: it was me who insisted that Sarah finally get around to reading *Hygiene And The Assassin* by Amélie Nothomb.

To start with she said:

"Not on your life! I don't like bestselling authors.

Plus I've seen that girl eating revolting things on telly!"
   She couldn't put that book down in the end . . .

I haven't left my studio since this morning and I'm writing even more fervently than before. It must be two or three o'clock in the afternoon.

I got a phone call from work yesterday. It was Mr Courgette, the grumpy-guts from human resources. I recognised his voice because it sounds like a broken guitar string:

"Do you recall that you've still got a job at our printing works?"

I hadn't been there for weeks. I'd given the excuse of my paternal aunt dying, then I'd added that I had a serious disease which the doctors couldn't diagnose and only the healers from back home could treat.

"Now listen here, you have already buried several members of your family in under six months, and it's been three times now that the same aunt has kicked the bucket!"

Seeing as I'd forgotten about recycling the same lies several times over, I tried to dig myself out:

"Mr Courgette, perhaps I didn't express myself very clearly, I'm talking about a different aunt . . . In Africa we have so many aunts we've got them coming out of our ears and sometimes they die in the same week, in the same place, in the same house and nobody bats an eyelid . . ."

"Look, we're just wasting time here, when are you coming back to work?"

"I've still got this disease the doctors can't . . ."

"Fine, go right ahead and be ill for a hundred years! I no longer require the services of a sluggard like you!"

I said that was fine by me, that next week I'd come and collect my gloves, my overalls and my hat because I was the one who'd bought them and there was no chance of me leaving my belongings to a capitalist who refused to make work tools available to his employees. Plus it was his job to sack me, not mine to hand in my notice!

* * *

Sarah came over to mine at the start of the evening and caught me in the middle of a writing frenzy.

"Where are you up to?" she asked me.

"I'm nearly at the end," I replied, not sounding very convinced.

For the first time since we've known each other, she picked up a few pages that were on the floor and starting reading them out loud. It was a tough test for me, my throat suddenly went very dry. I was worried my words wouldn't belong to me any more, that they would escape from the pages to die between Sarah's lips. I wanted to explain to her that I hadn't got a clean version yet, that Louis-Philippe hadn't read the manuscript, that it was still a first draft, that this or that was still missing. Too late, she carried on reading, her expression became more and more serious, she'd found my description of Original Colour, of her dark skin . . .

She tidied up the pages, put them down by my typewriter and said to me:

"There's a big problem in your *Black Bazaar* . . ."

"Oh yes?"

"Is my colour also an original colour?"

She burst out laughing and then she looked at me in this serious way I'd never seen before.

"I was waiting for you to finish your book," she whispered, "so I could say: I'd like you to come and live with me . . ."

Sarah Ardizzone was born in Brussels in 1970. She currently lives in Brixton, London. She won the Scott Moncrieff Prize for her translation of *Just Like Tomorrow* by the young French-Algerian writer Faïza Guène. While training in theatre in Paris she lived on the Rue Myrha opposite the Marché Dejean, where much of the action of *Black Bazaar* is set.

# Acknowledgements

The translator would like to thank Anna Shepherd, Milly Taylor and Emma Tubman, without whom . . .

Also, Daniel Boulland and Alison James-Moran for the Rue Myrha days.